W9-BIG-548

Madame Maigret pushed open the door, panting and flustered with her hat on crooked. She was an hour late. Maigret, dinnerless, was eating a hunk of cheese and bread. Her lips trembled.

### "Whatever happens, don't laugh."

And then she proceeded to tell a strange story —so strange that it was to lead Inspector Maigret along a devious, dangerous path, straight to the solution of an "impossible" crime.

> "Never before has Madame Maigret been involved in one of her famous inspector-husband's cases, but so successful is her initial adventure in this delightful Parisian murder story that no doubt M. Simenon will have to bring her back for encores."—*Fort Worth Star-Telegram*

## ABOUT THE AUTHOR

Georges Simenon was born on February 13, 1903, a good Friday the thirteenth for mystery fans. Born in Liége, Belgium, he was forced to stop his schooling at the age of sixteen because of the death of his father. He presented himself to the editor of a local paper, who hired him as a lark. Simenon has been writing ever since.

At the age of seventeen, he published his first novel. At twenty, he married and moved to Paris and, in the ensuing ten years, published some two hundred novels under sixteen pseudonyms. At thirty, on board his yacht, the *Ostrogot,* he wrote his first detective novel, creating the now-famous Inspector Maigret.

For the next two years he wrote a novel in the Maigret series every month, and is still penning an average of two Maigrets a year. Now residing in America, it is estimated by *Time* that he has published some 350 books.

# Madame Maigret's Own Case

# Own Case

# georges SIMENON

PYRAMID BOOKS  NEW YORK

**MADAME MAIGRET'S OWN CASE**

A PYRAMID BOOK

Published by arrangement with Doubleday & Company, Inc.

Pyramid edition published February 1963
    Second printing, March 1971

Library of Congress Catalog Card Number: 59-15002

Printed in the United States of America

PYRAMID BOOKS are published by Pyramid Publications
A Division of The Walter Reade Organization, Inc.
444 Madison Avenue, New York, New York 10022, U.S.A.

# 1

## THE NICE LADY
## IN THE PLACE D'ANVERS

THE CHICKEN WAS on the stove, with a fine red carrot, a big onion, and a bunch of parsley with the stems sticking out. Madame Maigret bent over to make sure there was no risk that the gas, which she had turned down as low as possible, would go out. Then she closed the windows, except for the one in the bedroom, checked to be sure she hadn't forgotten anything, glanced at the mirror and, satisfied, left the apartment, locked the door and put the key in her purse.

It was a little after ten o'clock on a March morning. The air was crisp, with sparkling sunshine over Paris. By walking as far as the Place de la République she could have taken a bus going right to the Boulevard Barbès and reached the Place d'Anvers in plenty of time for her eleven o'clock appointment.

Because of the "nice lady" she went down the stairs to the Richard-Lenoir métro station, just a step or two from her own door, and made the whole trip underground, at every stop looking vaguely at the familiar posters on the cream-colored walls.

Maigret had made fun of her, though not too much, for he had had a lot on his mind the last three weeks.

"Are you sure there isn't a good dentist nearer home?"

Madame Maigret had never before had any trouble with her teeth. Madame Roblin, the neighbor on the fourth floor—the one with the dog—had spoken so highly of Dr. Floresco that she had decided to go and see him.

"He has the fingers of a pianist. You won't even know he's working in your mouth. And as you're recommended by me he'll only charge you half the usual fee."

He was a Rumanian who had his office on the third floor of a building on the corner of the Rue Turgot and the Avenue Trudaine, exactly opposite the Place d'Anvers. Was this Madame Maigret's seventh or eighth visit? She had a regular appointment at eleven o'clock. It had become routine.

The first time, she had arrived a good quarter of an hour early, thanks to her morbid fear of keeping anyone waiting, and had twiddled her thumbs in a room overheated by a gas radiator. On her second visit she had also had to wait. Both times it was a quarter past eleven before she had been admitted to the dentist's office.

On the day of her third appointment, since there was bright sunshine and the square opposite was twittering with birds, she had decided to sit down on a bench and wait. This was how she had made the acquaintance of the lady with the little boy.

By now the habit was so well established that she deliberately left early and took the métro in order to save time.

It was pleasant to see grass, and buds already nearly bursting on the branches of the few trees outlined against the wall of the high school. Sitting in full sunshine on the bench, one could follow the movements of the Boulevard Rochechouart: the green and white buses, which looked like huge beasts, and the taxis darting in and out.

There was the lady, in a blue suit, just as on the other mornings, with her little white hat which was so becoming to her and so springlike. She slid over to make more room for Madame Maigret, who had brought a chocolate bar with her and held it out to the child.

"Say thank you, dear."

He was two, and the most striking thing about him was his big black eyes with immense lashes which made him look like a girl. At first Madame Maigret had wondered whether he could talk, whether the syllables he uttered belonged to any language. Then she had realized, though she hadn't gone so far as to ask their nationality, that he and the lady were foreigners.

"To me March is the most beautiful month in Paris, in spite of the showers," Madame Maigret was saying. "Some people prefer May or June, but March has so much more freshness."

She turned around from time to time to keep an eye on the dentist's window, for from where she was sitting she could see the head of the patient who usually preceded her. He was a man of about fifty, rather unfriendly, who was in the process of having all his teeth out. She had become acquainted with him too. He had been born in Dunkirk, lived with his married daughter in this neighborhood, but didn't like his son-in-law.

The little boy, equipped this morning with a tiny red bucket and spade, was playing with the gravel. He was always very clean, very well cared for.

"I think I'll only have to come twice more," Madame Maigret sighed. "According to what Dr. Floresco told me, he's going to start on the last tooth today."

The lady smiled as she listened. She spoke excellent French, with a trace of accent which lent it charm. At six or seven minutes to eleven she was still smiling at the child, who was greatly taken aback at having thrown dust in his own face; then all of a sudden she seemed to be looking at something in the Avenue Trudaine, to be hesitating. Then she stood up, saying urgently:

"Will you watch him for a minute? I'll be right back."

At the time Madame Maigret wasn't too surprised. With her appointment in mind, she simply hoped the mother would be back in time and tactfully refrained from turning around to see where she was going.

The little boy hadn't noticed anything. He was still squatting there, playing at filling his red bucket with pebbles, emptying it and indomitably starting all over again.

Madame Maigret wasn't wearing a watch. Her watch hadn't run for years, and she never remembered to take it to the watchmaker. An old man came and sat down on the bench; he must have been a resident of the neighborhood, for she had seen him before.

"Would you be kind enough to tell me the time, monsieur?"

He must not have had a watch either, because he only answered:

"About eleven o'clock."

The head was no longer to be seen in the dentist's window. Madame Maigret was beginning to be anxious. She was ashamed to keep Dr. Floresco waiting; he was so nice, so gentle, and his patience was unfailing.

She looked all around the square without seeing the young lady in the white hat. Had she suddenly been taken ill? Or had she seen someone she wanted to speak to?

A policeman was walking through the square, and Madame Maigret stood up to ask him the time. It really was eleven o'clock.

The lady still did not come back, and the minutes were going by. The child had looked up at the bench and seen that his mother was no longer there, but he hadn't seemed to mind.

If only Madame Maigret could get in touch with the dentist! She would only have to cross the street and go up three flights of stairs. Now she felt tempted to ask the old gentleman to watch the little boy while she went up to explain to Dr. Floresco, but she didn't like to and she remained standing up, looking around her with mounting impatience.

The second time she asked a passer-by the time, it was twenty past eleven. The old gentleman had gone. She was alone now on the bench. She had seen the patient who preceded her come out of the corner building and walk off in the direction of the Rue Rochechouart.

What should she do? Had something happened to the nice lady? If she had been knocked down by a car she would have seen a crowd, people running. Was the child going to get upset now perhaps?

It was a ridiculous situation. Maigret would make fun of her again. It would be best not to mention it to him. She would telephone the dentist in a little while and apologize. Would she dare to tell him what had happened?

Suddenly she felt hot because her nervousness was making her blood tingle.

"What's your name?" she asked the child.

But he just looked at her out of his dark eyes without answering.

"Do you know where you live?"

He wasn't listening to her. It had already occurred to Madame Maigret that he might not understand French.

"Excuse me, monsieur. Could you tell me the time, please?"

"Twenty-two minutes to twelve, madame."

There was no sign of the mother. At noon, when whistles blew in the vicinity and a nearby bar was invaded by bricklayers, she still hadn't returned.

Dr. Floresco came out of the building and got behind the wheel of a small black car, yet she did not dare to leave the child to go and apologize.

What was on her mind now was her chicken, still on

the stove. Maigret had told her that he would more than likely be home to lunch at about one.

Ought she to inform the police? In any case to do so she would have to leave the square. If she took the child with her and the mother came back in the meantime she would be out of her mind with anxiety. Goodness knows where she would run off to then or where they would finally catch up with each other! But she couldn't leave a two-year-old baby alone in the middle of a square either, just a step or two from the buses and cars which were passing in a steady stream.

"Excuse me, monsieur. Would you tell me what time it is?"

"Half past twelve."

The chicken was certainly beginning to burn; Maigret would be coming in. It would be the first time in all these years of marriage that he hadn't found her at home.

It was impossible to telephone him, either, because she would have to leave the square and go into a bar. If only she could see that policeman who had gone past, or any policeman, she would tell him who she was and ask him to be kind enough to call her husband. As if it had been deliberately arranged, there wasn't one in sight. She looked in all directions; sat down; stood up again; kept thinking she saw the white hat; but it was never the one she was waiting for.

She counted more than twenty white hats in half an hour, and four of them were worn by women in blue suits.

\* \* \*

At eleven o'clock, while Madame Maigret was beginning to be worried, detained in the middle of the square by responsibility for a child whose name she didn't even know, Maigret was putting on his hat, leaving his office, addressing a few words to Lucas and walking glumly toward the

little door which connects the offices of the Police Judiciaire with the Palais de Justice.

It had become a routine, dating from about the time
Madame Maigret went to see her dentist in the Ninth
Arrondissement. The chief inspector entered the examining magistrates' corridor, where there were always some
queer-looking birds waiting on the benches, some of them
flanked by policemen, and knocked at the door that bore
the name of Judge Dossin.

"Come in."

Monsieur Dossin was the tallest magistrate in Paris and
he always seemed to be embarrassed about it and to be
apologizing for having the aristocratic figure of a Russian
wolfhound.

"Sit down, Maigret. Smoke your pipe. Have you read
this morning's article?"

"I haven't seen the papers yet."

The magistrate pushed one over to him with a big front-
page headline which read:

## STEUVELS CASE

### Maître Philippe Liotard Appeals
### to the League for Human Rights

"I've had a long talk with the Public Prosecutor," said
Dossin. "He agrees with me. We can't release the bookbinder. Even if we wanted to, Liotard himself would prevent us by his virulence."

A few weeks ago this name had been practically unknown at the Palais. Philippe Liotard, who was not much
over thirty, had never pleaded an important case. After
having been an assistant to a famous lawyer for five years,
he was just setting up for himself and still lived in a
bachelor apartment devoid of prestige in the Rue Bergère,
next door to a house of ill fame.

Ever since the Steuvels case had broken he was mentioned in the papers every day, gave sensational interviews, issued communiqués, even appeared on movie screens in newsreels, his forelock belligerent, his smile sarcastic.

"Nothing new with you?"

"Nothing worth reporting, Monsier le Juge."

"Do you hope to find the man who handed in the telegram?"

"Torrence is at Concarneau. He's a resourceful fellow."

In the three weeks it had held public opinion in its grip the Steuvels case had already run through a certain number of subheads like a newspaper serial.

It had begun with:

### THE CELLAR IN THE RUE DE TURENNE

By chance it happened that the setting was a district which Maigret knew well, in which he even had a hankering to live, less than fifty yards from the Place des Vosges.

Leaving the narrow Rue des Francs-Bourgeois at the corner of the square and following the Rue de Turenne toward the République, you come first, on the left, to a yellow-painted bistro, then to a little restaurant, the Crémerie Salmon. Right next door is a glass-fronted studio with a low ceiling and a dusty show window on which is written in tarnished letters: *Art Binding*. In the shop next door Madame Veuve Rancé runs an umbrella business.

Between the studio and the umbrella shopwindow is the main entrance, under an archway housing the concierge's apartment, and, at the rear of the courtyard, an old town house, now riddled with offices and apartments.

### A BODY IN THE FURNACE?

What the public didn't know, what had been carefully kept from the press, was that it was through sheer chance that the case had come to light. One morning in the mailbox at Police Headquarters had been found a dirty slip of wrapping paper on which was written:

> The bookbinder in the Rue de Turenne has
> burned a body in his furnace.

It wasn't signed, obviously. The paper had wound up on Maigret's desk; skeptical, he hadn't bothered one of his veteran inspectors with it but had sent little Lapointe, a young man who was itching to distinguish himself.

Lapointe had discovered that there was indeed a bookbinder in the Rue de Turenne, a man from Flanders resident in France for more than twenty-five years, Frans Steuvels. Posing as a sanitary inspector, the detective had been through his premises and returned with a detailed plan.

"Steuvels work in the shopwindow, so to speak, Chief Inspector. The rear of the workshop, which gets darker as you get farther back from the street, is cut off by a wooden partition behind which the Steuvelses have fixed up their bedroom.

"A staircase leads to the basement, where there is a kitchen, plus a small room, where they have to keep the light on all day, which serves as a dining room, and finally a cellar."

"With a furnace?"

"Yes. An old model which doesn't seem to be in very good shape."

"Does it work?"

"It wasn't going this morning."

It was Lucas who had gone to the Rue de Turenne at about five o'clock in the afternoon for an official search. Fortunately he had taken a warrant with him, because the bookbinder had claimed the inviolability of domicile.

Sergeant Lucas had nearly gone away empty-handed, and now that the case had turned into a nightmare for the Police Judiciaire they were inclined to resent his partial success.

Sifting the ashes at the very back of the furnace, he had

come upon two teeth, two human teeth, which he had immediately taken to the laboratory.

"What kind of man is he, this bookbinder?" Maigret had asked. At that point he was only remotely connected with the case.

"He must be about forty-five. He's red-haired, pock-marked, with blue eyes and a very gentle expression. His wife, although she's younger than he is, never takes her eyes off him, as if he were a child."

They knew by now that Fernande, who had become notorious too, had come to Paris as a domestic servant and later had been on the streets for several years along the Boulevard de Sébastopol.

She was thirty-six; had been living with Steuvels for ten years; and three years ago, for no apparent reason, they had been married at the town hall of the Third Arrondissement.

The laboratory had sent up its report. The teeth were those of a man of about thirty, probably fairly fat, who must still have been alive a few days earlier.

Steuvels had been brought into Maigret's office, amicably, and the grilling had begun. He was sitting in the green plush armchair facing the window which overlooked the Seine, and that evening it was pouring. Throughout the ten or twelve hours the interrogation had lasted, they had heard the rain beating against the windowpanes and the gurgling of water in the gutter. The bookbinder wore spectacles with thick lenses and steel rims. His abundant, rather long hair was shaggy, and his tie was crooked.

He was a cultured man who had read a lot. He remained calm and deliberate; his delicate, ruddy skin flushed easily.

"How do you explain the fact that human teeth have been found in your furnace?"

"I don't explain it."

"Have you lost any teeth recently? Or your wife?"

"Neither one of us. Mine are false."

He had taken his plate out of his mouth, then put it back with a practiced movement.

"Can you give me an account of how you spent the evenings of February 16, 17 and 18?"

The interrogation was taking place on the evening of the twenty-first, after the visits of Lapointe and Lucas to the Rue de Turenne.

"Do those dates include a Friday?"

"The sixteenth."

"In that case I went to the Saint-Paul movie house in the Rue Saint-Antoine, as I do every Friday."

"With your wife?"

"Yes."

"And the other two days?"

"It was Saturday afternoon that Fernande left."

"Where did she go?"

"To Concarneau."

"Had the trip been planned long beforehand?"

"Her mother, who's a cripple, lives with her daughter and son-in-law at Concarneau. On Saturday morning we received a telegram from the sister, Louise, saying that their mother was seriously ill, and Fernande took the first train."

"Without telephoning?"

"They have no telephone."

"Was the mother very bad?"

"She wasn't ill at all. The telegram didn't come from Louise."

"Who did it come from then?"

"We don't know."

"Have tricks of this kind ever been played on you before?"

"No. Never."

"When did your wife get back?"

"On the Tuesday. She took advantage of being down there to spend a couple of days with her family."

"What did you do all that time?"

"I worked."

"One of the tenants states that dense smoke was coming out of your chimney all day on the Sunday."

"That's possible. It was cold."

This was true. The Sunday and Monday had been very cold days, and severe frost had been predicted in the suburbs.

"What suit were you wearing on Saturday evening?"

"The same one I'm wearing today."

"Did anyone come to see you after you closed?"

"Nobody except a client who called for a book. Do you want his name and address?"

It was a well-known man, a member of the Hundred Bibliophiles. Thanks to Liotard, more was to be heard of these men, who were nearly all important personalities.

"Your concierge, Madame Salazar, heard someone knock at your door that evening about nine o'clock. Several people were talking excitedly."

"People talking on the sidewalk perhaps, but not inside my place. It's entirely possible, if they were excited, as Madame Salazar claims, that they knocked against the window."

"How many suits do you own?"

"As I have only one body and one head, I own only one suit and one hat, apart from the old trousers and sweater I wear for work."

He had then been shown a navy-blue suit found in the wardrobe in his bedroom.

"What about this one?"

"That doesn't belong to me."

"How does this suit happen to have been found in your room?"

"I've never seen it. Anybody might have put it there in my absence. I've been here six hours already."

"Do you mind slipping on the coat?"

It fitted him.

"Do you see these stains which look like rust? It's blood, human blood, according to the experts. Futile attempts have been made to get rid of them."

"I don't recognize this clothing."

"Madame Rancé, the umbrella woman, states that she often saw you wearing blue, especially on Fridays, when you were going to the movies."

"I did have another suit, and it was blue, but I got rid of it more than two months ago."

After this first interrogation Maigret was gloomy. He had had a long conversation with Judge Dossin, after which both of them had gone to see the Public Prosecutor.

It was the latter who had assumed responsibility for the arrest.

"The experts are in agreement, aren't they? The rest, Maigret, is up to you. Go ahead. We can't release that customer."

By the next day Maître Liotard had emerged from the shadows, and, ever since, Maigret had had him at his heels like a snapping mongrel.

Among the newspaper subheads there had been one that had had quite a success:

### THE PHANTOM SUITCASE

Young Lapointe declared, in fact, that when he had looked around the premises as the alleged sanitary inspector he had seen a reddish-brown suitcase under a table in the workshop.

"It was an ordinary cheap suitcase, and I stumbled into it. I was surprised it hurt so much and I realized why when I tried to lift it because it was unusually heavy."

Yet at five in the afternoon, the time of the search by Lucas, the suitcase was no longer there. To be more precise, there was still a suitcase, also brown and also cheap, but Lapointe maintained that it was not the same one.

"That's the suitcase I took to Concarneau," Fernande had said. "We've never owned another one. We hardly travel at all."

Lapointe was unshakable, swore it was not the same suitcase, that the first one was lighter in color and had its handle tied up with string.

"If I had had a suitcase to mend," retorted Steuvels, "I wouldn't have used string. Don't forget that I'm a bookbinder and a skilled leather worker."

Then Philippe Liotard had started collecting testimonials from bibliophiles, and it had turned out that Steuvels was one of the best bookbinders in Paris, possibly the best, and that collectors entrusted their delicate work to him, especially the restoration of antique bindings.

Everybody agreed that he was an even-tempered man who spent practically his whole life in his workshop, and the police were raking through his past to no avail in search of the slightest equivocal detail.

True, there was that item of Fernande. He had known her when she was on the streets, and it was he who had taken her away from all that. But there was absolutely nothing against Fernande either, since that period back in the past.

Torrence had been at Concarneau for four days. At the post office the original of the telegram had been found, printed by hand in block letters. The postmistress thought she remembered that it was a woman who had handed it across the counter, and Torrence was still searching, compiling a list of recent arrivals from Paris, questioning two hundred people a day.

"We are fed up with the so-called infallibility of Chief Inspector Maigret!" Maître Liotard had declared to a journalist.

And he made reference to some trouble in a local election in the Third Arrondissement which might well have induced certain people to precipitate a scandal in the district for political ends.

Judge Dossin, too, was getting it in the neck, and these attacks, not always subtle, made him blush.

"You haven't a single new clue?"

"I'm still looking. There are ten of us looking—sometimes more—and we're interrogating some people for the twentieth time. Lucas is hoping to find the tailor who made the blue suit."

As always happens when a case arouses popular opinion, they were receiving hundreds of letters a day, almost all of which sent them off on false trails, causing them to waste a great deal of time. Nevertheless, everything was scrupulously checked, and even lunatics who claimed to know something were given a hearing.

At ten minutes to one Maigret got out of the bus on the corner of the Boulevard Voltaire and, glancing up at his windows as he always did, was a little surprised to see that the one in the dining room was closed, in spite of the bright sun shining directly on it.

He walked heavily upstairs and turned the doorknob, which didn't yield. Occasionally, when Madame Maigret was dressing or undressing, she would lock the door. He opened it with his own key, found himself in a cloud of blue smoke and dashed into the kitchen to turn off the gas. In the casserole all that was left of the chicken, carrot and onion was a scorched crust.

He opened all the windows, and when a panting Madame Maigret pushed open the door half an hour later she found him sitting there with a hunk of bread and a piece of cheese.

"What time is it?"

"Half past one," he said calmly.

He had never seen her in such a state: her hat was crooked, her lip quivered tremulously.

"Whatever happens, don't laugh."

"I'm not laughing."

"Don't scold me either. I couldn't help it and I'd like to have seen you in my position. And to think that you're reduced to eating a piece of cheese for lunch!"

"The dentist?"

"I haven't seen the dentist. Since a quarter to eleven I've been in the middle of the Place d'Anvers, without budging."

"Were you taken ill?"

"Have I ever been taken ill in my life? No, it was because of the baby. And in the end, when he began to cry and create a scene, there I was looking like a kidnaper."

"What baby? A baby what?"

"I told you about the lady in blue and her child, but you never do listen to me. The one I met on the bench while I was waiting for the dentist. This morning she suddenly got up and went off, asking me to watch the child for a moment."

"And she didn't come back? What did you do with the boy?"

"She finally did come back, just a quarter of an hour ago. I came home in a taxi."

"What did she say when she came back?"

"To crown it all she didn't even speak to me. I was in the middle of the square, stuck there like a scarecrow, with the little boy yelling fit to draw a crowd.

"I finally saw a taxi stopping on the corner of the Avenue Trudaine and I recognized the white hat. She didn't even bother to get out. She opened the door and beckoned to me. The child was running ahead of me, and I was afraid he'd get run over. He reached the taxi first, and the door was closing again by the time I got there.

" 'Tomorrow,' she called. 'I'll explain tomorrow. Forgive me. . . .'

"She didn't thank me. The taxi was already going off in

the direction of the Boulevard Rochechouart and it turned
left toward Pigalle."

She stopped, out of breath, took off her hat with such
a brusque movement that she rumpled her hair.

"Are you laughing?"

"Of course not."

"You may as well admit that it makes you laugh. All
the same she did leave her child in charge of a stranger for
more than two hours. She doesn't even know my name."

"And you? Do you know hers?"

"No."

"Do you know where she lives?"

"I don't know anything at all except that I missed my
appointment, my good chicken is ruined, and you're eating
a piece of cheese off a corner of the table like a—like
a——"

Then, not able to find the word, she began to cry, walking toward the bedroom door to change her dress.

# 2

## THE WORRIES OF THE GREAT TURENNE

MAIGRET HAD A MANNER all his own of climbing the two flights of stairs at the Quai des Orfèvres: his expression remained pretty indifferent at first, at the foot of the staircase, where the light from outside struck it almost full strength, then it grew more and more preoccupied the deeper he penetrated into the gray shadows of the old building, as though office worries thrust themselves more heavily upon him as he drew nearer to them.

By the time he passed the usher he was already the chief. Recently he had got into the habit, both morning and afternoon, before pushing open his own door, of stopping by the inspectors' office and, his hat on his head, his overcoat on his back, going in to see The Great Turenne.

This was the latest gag at headquarters, and it was indicative of the stature the Steuvels case had attained. Lucas, who had been forced to take charge of centralizing information, collating it and keeping it up to date, had quickly been swamped, for it was also his job to answer telephone calls, open all mail concerning the case and interview informants.

Incapable of working in the inspectors' office, where there was constant coming and going, he had taken refuge in an adjoining room, on the door of which a facetious hand had written: "The Great Turenne."

As soon as a detective had finished an assignment, as soon as anyone came back from a job, a colleague would ask him:

"Are you free?"

"Yes."

"Go in and see The Great Turenne. He's hiring!"

It was true. Little Lucas never had enough staff for all the checks he had to make, and there was probably nobody left in the department who hadn't been sent out at least once to the Rue de Turenne.

They all knew the intersection near the bookbinder's studio, with the three cafés: first the café-restaurant on the corner of the Rue des Francs-Bourgeois, then the Grand Turenne opposite, and finally, a hundred feet away, on the corner of the Place des Vosges, the Tabac des Vosges, which the newspapermen had adopted as their headquarters. Because they were in on the case too.

The detectives, for their part, took their drinks at the Grand Turenne, from the windows of which you could see the studio of the Flemish bookbinder. This was *their* headquarters, and Lucas' office had turned into a sort of local branch.

The most amazing thing was that good old Lucas, chained down by his classification work, was probably the only one who still hadn't set foot on the scene of action since his visit there the first day.

Nevertheless, it was he who knew that corner better than any of them. He knew that after the Grand Turenne (the café!) came a high-class wineshop, Les Caves de Bourgogne, and he was acquainted with its proprietors; he needed only to consult a card to find out what they had told every interrogator.

No. They hadn't seen anything. But on Saturday evenings they left for the Chevreuse Valley, where they spent the weekend in a cabin they had built themselves.

After Les Caves de Bourgogne came the shop of a shoe-maker named Bousquet.

He, on the other hand, talked too much; only he had the defect of not telling everybody the same thing. It depended on what time of day he was questioned, how many apéritifs and brandies he had had at one of the three cafés, no matter which.

Then came Frère's stationery business, semi-wholesale; and at the rear, in the courtyard, there was a manufacturer of cardboard.

Above Frans Steuvels' studio, on the second floor of the old town house, jewelry was mass-produced. This was the firm of Sass & Lapinsky, which employed about twenty girls and four or five men, the latter all with outlandish names.

Everybody had been questioned, some of them four or five times, by various inspectors, not to mention the numerous inquiries of the reporters. Two pine tables in Lucas' office were covered with papers, plans, memos, and he was the only man who could find his way around in the muddle.

And indefatigably Lucas went on bringing his notes up to date. Once more this afternoon Maigret took up his position behind Lucas' back, not saying anything, pulling gently on his pipe.

A page headed "Motives" was black with notes which had been crossed out one by one.

They had looked for a political angle. Not in the direction Maître Liotard had indicated because that wouldn't hold up. But Steuvels, who lived like a recluse, might have belonged to some subversive organization.

This hadn't led anywhere. The deeper they looked into his life the more realized that it was unexceptional. The books in his library, examined one by one, were books selected from the best writers of the whole world by an intelligent, unusually cultured man. Not only did he read and reread them, but he made notes in the margins.

Jealousy? Fernande never went out without him except to do her marketing in the neighborhood, and from where he sat he could almost keep an eye on her in all the shops where she traded.

They had wondered if there might be a connection between the presumed murder and the proximity of Messrs. Sass & Lapinsky. Nothing had been stolen from the jewelry manufacturers. Neither the owner nor the employees knew the bookbinder, except by sight behind his window.

Nothing from the Belgian angle either. Steuvels had left there at the age of eighteen and had never been back. He wasn't interested in politics, and there was no indication that he might belong to a Flemish extremist movement.

They had thought of everything. Lucas was accepting the craziest suggestions as a matter of duty. He would open the door of the inspectors' office and call one of them at random.

They knew what that meant. A new check to be made, in the Rue de Turenne or somewhere else.

"I may have got hold of something," he said to Maigret this time, pouncing on a sheet of paper among the scattered files. "I've had a notice sent out to all taxi drivers. One's just left, a naturalized Russian. I'll get it checked."

This was the current word: *Check!*

"I wanted to find out whether a taxi had brought anybody to the bookbinder's after dark on Saturday, February 17. The driver, by the name of Georges Peskine, was hailed by three people that Saturday at about quarter past eight near the Gare Saint-Lazare, and they told him to take them to the corner of the Rue de Turenne and the Rue des Francs-Bourgeois. So it was after half past eight when he dropped them, which doesn't fit too badly with the concierge's testimony about the noise she heard. The driver doesn't know who his fares were. But, according to him, the one who seemed the most important of the three, the one who spoke to him, was a Levantine."

"What language were they speaking to each other?"

"French. One of the others, a big, fair, rather heavy man of around thirty, blessed with a strong Hungarian accent, seemed to be worried, uneasy. The third, a middle-aged Frenchman, not so well dressed as his companions, didn't seem quite up to them socially.

"When they got out of the cab the Levantine paid, and all three of them walked back up the Rue de Turenne toward the bookbinder's."

If it hadn't been for this business of the taxi Maigret might never have thought of his wife's adventure.

"While you're working on the taxi drivers you might just inquire about a little incident that happened this morning. It hasn't anything to do with our case, but it intrigues me."

Lucas wasn't prepared to be so sure that it had nothing to do with his case, for he was ready to connect the remotest, most fortuitous events with it. First thing every morning he had all the metropolitan police reports sent up to him to make sure they didn't contain anything that might come within his field of activity.

All alone in his office he was coping with an enormous work load of which the public, reading the papers and following the Steuvels case like a serial, had not the least inkling.

Maigret briefly sketched the episode of the lady in the white hat and the little boy.

"You might also call the Ninth Arrondissement police. The fact that she was on the same bench in the Place d'Anvers park every morning makes it seem likely that she lives in their neighborhood. Let them check that whole area, the tradesmen, the hotels and rooming houses."

Check, check! In normal times you could sometimes find ten inspectors at a time smoking, preparing reports, reading newspapers or even playing cards in the next office.

Now you almost never saw two at once. Scarcely had they come in than The Great Turenne would open the door of his den.

"Are you free, son? Come in here a minute."

And one or more of them would set off on a trail.

The vanished suitcase had been hunted in the baggage rooms of all the stations and in all the junk shops.

Little Lapointe may have been inexperienced, but he was a responsible young man, incapable of making up a story.

On the morning of February 21, therefore, there must have been in Steuvels' workshop a suitcase that was no longer there when Lucas appeared at five o'clock.

Yet so far as the neighbors could recollect Steuvels had not left home that day, and no one had seen Fernande go out with a suitcase or package.

Had anyone come to call for any binding work? This had also been "checked." The Argentine embassy had sent for a document for which Steuvels had created a sumptuous binding, but it was not bulky, and the messenger had it under his arm when he left.

Martin, the most cultured man at Police Headquarters, had worked for almost a week in the bookbinder's shop, examining his books, studying the work he had turned out during the last few months, getting in touch with his clients by telephone.

"He's an amazing man," was his conclusion. "He has the most select clientele you can imagine. They all have complete confidence in him. What's more, he works for several embassies."

But this angle yielded nothing mysterious either. If the embassies entrusted their work to him it was because he was a specialist in heraldry and owned the stamps for a large number of coats of arms, which enabled him to bind books or documents emblazoned with the arms of various countries.

"You don't look happy, Chief. But you'll see. Something will emerge out of all this in the end."

And good old Lucas, who never lost heart, pointed to the hundreds of sheets of paper he was blithely accumulating.

"We found some teeth in the furnace, didn't we? They didn't get there all by themselves. And someone handed in a telegram at Concarneau to lure Steuvels' wife down there. The blue suit hanging in the wardrobe had human bloodstains on it which someone had tried unsuccessfully to remove. Maître Liotard can talk and carry on until he's blue in the face; he won't budge me on that."

But all this paper work, so intoxicating to the detective, overwhelmed the chief inspector, who was looking at it with a jaundiced eye.

"What are you thinking about, Chief?"

"Nothing. I'm wondering."

"About releasing him?"

"No. That's the examining magistrate's business."

"Otherwise you'd have him released, wouldn't you?"

"I don't know. I'm wondering whether to start the whole case over again from the beginning."

"Just as you like," replied Lucas, slightly offended.

"That doesn't prevent you from going ahead with your work. On the contrary. If we wait too long we'll never get it straight. It's always the same: once the press interferes, everybody has something to say, and we're swamped."

"All the same I've found the taxi driver, just as I'm going to find Madame Maigret's."

The chief inspector filled a fresh pipe, opened the door. There wasn't a single detective next door. They had all gone off somewhere, busy with the man from Flanders.

"Have you made up your mind?"

"I think so."

He didn't even go into his own office but left the Quai des Orfèvres and immediately hailed a cab.

"Corner of the Rue de Turenne and the Rue des Francs-Bourgeois."

Those words, which you kept hearing from morning to night, were becoming revolting.

\* \* \*

The residents of the neighborhood, for their part, had never had such a time. All of them, one after the other, had had their names in the paper. Shopkeepers, workmen—all they had to do was drop into the Grand Turenne for a drink and they met the detectives, and if they went across the street to the Tabac des Vosges, which was famous for its white wine, they were greeted by reporters.

Ten times, twenty times, they had been asked their opinion of Steuvels, of Fernande, and for details about their movements.

Since there wasn't even a body when all was said and done—nothing but two teeth—the whole thing was not at all tragic and seemed more like a game.

Maigret left the cab opposite the Grand Turenne, glanced inside, saw no one from the department, walked a few steps and found himself in front of the bookbinder's studio, where the shutters had been up and the door closed for the last three weeks. There was no bell, and he knocked, knowing that Fernande ought to be at home.

It was in the morning that she went out. Every day since the arrest of Frans, in fact, she had left at ten o'clock, carying three small casseroles which fitted into one another and were held by a frame surmounted by a handle. It was her husband's meals that she carried to the Santé prison in this way, by métro.

Maigret knocked a second time and saw her emerge from the stairway which connected the workshop with the basement. She recognized him, turned around to speak to someone out of sight, and finally came to let him in.

She was in slippers and wore a checkered apron. Seeing her like this, a bit overweight, her face bare of make-up no one would have recognized the woman who once walked the little streets around the Boulevard de Sébastopol. She looked for all the world like a homebody, a meticulous housewife, and in normal times she was probably a cheerful soul.

"Is it me you want to see?" she asked, not without a suggestion of weariness.

"Is anyone with you?"

She did not answer, and Maigret walked over to the stairs and went down a few steps, then leaned over and frowned.

He had already been informed of the presence in the neighborhood of Alfonsi, who liked to drink an apéritif with the newspapermen in the Tabac des Vosges but avoided setting foot in the Grand Turenne.

He was standing, very much at home, in the kitchen, where something was simmering on the stove, and even though he was slightly embarrassed he managed an ironical smile for the chief inspector.

"What are you doing here?"

"You can see for yourself. Visiting. Just like you. I have a right to, haven't I?"

Alfonsi had been attached to the Police Judiciaire, but not in Maigret's department. For a few years he had been in the Vice Squad, where it had finally been made clear to him that in spite of all his political pull he was unwanted.

Short in stature, he wore very high heels to make himself taller, possibly with a deck of cards inside his shoes, as some people hinted, and he was always dressed with exaggerated elegance, a big diamond, genuine or paste, on his finger.

He had opened a private detective agency in the Rue Notre-Dame-de-Lorette of which he was both proprietor and sole employee, assisted only by a vague secretary who was primarily his mistress and with whom he was to be seen in the evenings in night clubs.

When Maigret had been told of his presence in the Rue de Turenne, the chief inspector had at first thought that the ex-detective was trying to pick up bits of information which he could later sell to newspapermen.

Then he had discovered that he was in the pay of Philippe Liotard.

It was the first time Maigret had crossed Alfonsi's path in person, and he muttered:

"I'm waititng."

"What are you waiting for?"

"For you to go."

"That's too bad because I'm not through."

"Suit yourself."

Maigret made as though to leave.

"What are you going to do?"

"Call one of my men and put a tail on you day and night. I have a right to, too."

"Okay. That's fine. No need to get nasty, Monsieur Maigret."

He set off up the stairs with his air of being quite at home in the underworld, winking at Fernande before he left.

"Does he come here often?" asked Maigret.

"This is the second time."

"I advise you not to trust him."

"I know. I know that type."

Was this a discreet allusion to the days when she was at the mercy of the men in the Vice Squad?

"How's Steuvels?"

"All right. He reads all day long. He's confident."

"And you?"

Was there really a hesitation?

"So am I."

Nonetheless she was obviously rather wary.

"What books are you taking him now?"

"He's in the middle of rereading Marcel Proust all the way through."

"Have you read him too?"

"Yes."

Steuvels had, in fact, educated the wife he had picked up long ago in the gutter.

"You mustn't think I've come to see you as an enemy. You know the situation as well as I do. I want to understand. For the time being I don't understand. Do you?"

"I'm sure Frans hasn't committed any crime."

"Do you love him?"

"That word doesn't mean anything. I'd need another word, a special one which doesn't exist."

He went up to the workshop again, where the bookbinder's tools were laid out on the long table facing the window. The presses were at the back, in semidarkness, and on the shelves books awaited their turn among the work in progress.

"He had regular habits, didn't he? I'd like you to tell me as accurately as possible how he spent his day."

"Somebody else has asked me that already."

"Who?"

"Maître Liotard."

"Has it occurred to you that Maître Liotard's interests don't necessarily coincide with your own? He was unknown three weeks ago and what he is after is to get as much publicity for his own name as possible. It doesn't matter to him whether your husband is innocent or guilty."

"Excuse me. If he proves his innocence, that will be a terrific boost for him, and his reputation will be made."

"And if he obtains your husband's release without having definitely proved his innocence? He'll make a name as a smart operator. He'll be in great demand. They'll say of your husband: 'Lucky for him Liotard got him off!' In other words, the guiltier Steuvels appears the more credit Liotard will get. Do you realize that?"

"Frans realizes it, anyhow."

"Did he say so?"

"Yes."

"Doesn't he like Liotard? why did he choose him?"

"He didn't choose him. Liotard himself——"

"Just a minute. You've just said something important."

"I know."

"Did you do it on purpose?"

"Maybe I did. I'm sick of all this fuss about us and I realize where it's coming from. It doesn't seem to me that I'm doing Frans any harm by saying what I'm saying."

"When Sergeant Lucas came to make his search on February 21 at about five o'clock he didn't leave alone but took your husband along with him."

"And you questioned him all night," she said reproachfully.

"That's my trade. At that time Steuvels still had no lawyer because he didn't know he was going to be held. And since then he hasn't been released. He came back here only for a very short time, accompanied by detectives. Yet when I told him to choose a lawyer he named Maître Liotard without any hesitation."

"I see what you mean."

"So the lawyer saw Steuvels here *before* Sergeant Lucas did?"

"Yes."

"Therefore it must have been on the afternoon of the twenty-first, between the visits of Lapointe and the sergeant?"

"Yes."

"Were you present at the interview?"

"I was downstairs doing a thorough cleaning, because I'd been away three days."

"You don't know what they said to each other? They hadn't met before?"

"No."

"It wasn't your husband who had telephoned to ask him to come?"

"I'm almost sure it wasn't."

Some children from the neighborhood had their faces pressed against the window, and Maigret suggested:

"Wouldn't you rather we went downstairs?"

She led him through the kitchen, and they entered the little windowless room, which was very attractive, very cozy, with shelves of books all around, the table at which the couple had their meals and, in a corner, another table, which served as a desk.

"You were asking me how my husband spent his time. He got up every day at six, winter and summer, and in winter the first thing he did was to go and stoke the furnace."

"Why wasn't it going on the twenty-first?"

"It wasn't cold enough. After a few freezing days the weather had turned mild again, and neither of us feels the cold much. In the kitchen I have the gas stove, which gives out enough heat, and there's another one in the studio that Frans uses for his glue and his tools.

"Before shaving he would go around to the bakery for croissants while I made the coffee, and we would have breakfast.

"Then he would wash up and get to work. I would leave the house about nine, having finished most of my housework, to do my marketing."

"He never went out to deliver work?"

"Hardly ever. People would bring their work to him and call for it. When he had to go out I used to go with him, because those were just about our only outings.

"We had lunch at half past twelve."

"Would he go back to work right away?"

"Nearly always, after spending a few minutes in the

doorway smoking a cigarette, because he didn't smoke while he was working.

"This would go on until seven o'clock, sometimes half past seven. I never knew what time we'd have dinner, because he always wanted to finish what he was working on. Then he would put up the shutters, wash his hands, and after dinner we would read, in this room, until ten or eleven o'clock. Except on Friday evenings, when we went to the Saint-Paul movie house."

"He didn't drink?"

"A glass of brandy every night after dinner. Just one little glass which would last him an hour, because he never took more than a sip at a time."

"And Sundays? Did you go to the country?"

"Never. He hated the country. We would loaf about all morning without getting dressed. He went in for carpentry a bit. He made these shelves himself and just about everything we have here. In the afternoons we'd go for a walk in the Francs-Bourgeois neighborhood or on the Ile Saint-Louis and we often had dinner at a little restaurant near the Pont Neuf."

"Is he stingy?"

She blushed and answered less spontaneously, with a question, as women do when they are embarrassed:

"Why do you ask me that?"

"He's been working at this rate for more than twenty years, hasn't he?"

"He's worked all his life. His mother was very poor. He had an unhappy childhood."

"And yet he's supposed to be the most expensive book-binder in Paris and he turns away more orders than he asks for."

"That's true."

"On what he makes you could live comfortably with a modern apartment and even a car."

"What for?"

"He maintains that he's never had more than one suit at a time, and your wardrobe doesn't seem any more extensive."

"I don't need anything. We eat well."

"You can't spend more than a third of what he earns for living expenses."

"I don't pay any attention to money matters."

"Most men work for some special goal. Some want a house in the country; others have dreams of retiring; others do it for the sake of their children. He had no children, had he?"

"Unfortunately I can't have any."

"And before your time?"

"No. He never knew any women, in a manner of speaking. He made do with you know what, and that's how I met him."

"What does he do with his money?"

"I don't know. I suppose he invests it."

They had, in fact, discovered a bank account in Steuvels' name at the Rue Saint-Antoine branch of the Société Générale. Nearly every week the bookbinder would deposit small sums which corresponded to the amounts received from clients.

"He worked for the pleasure of working. He comes from Flanders. I'm beginning to know what that means. He was capable of spending hours on a binding just for the joy of producing something out of the ordinary."

It was odd: sometimes she would speak of him in the past tense, as if the walls of the Santé prison had already cut him off from the world, sometimes in the present, as if he would be home any minute.

"Did he keep in touch with his family?"

"He never knew his father. He was brought up by an uncle who placed him in a charity institution when he was very young—luckily for him, because that's where he learned his trade. They were badly treated, and he doesn't like to talk about it."

There was no exit from the apartment except the studio door. To reach the courtyard it was necessary to go out into the street and through the archway, passing the concierge's apartment.

It was amazing, at the Quai des Orfèvres, to hear Lucas rattling off all these names, which Maigret could hardly keep straight: Madame Salazar, the concierge; Mademoiselle Béguin, the fifth-floor tenant; the shoemaker; the umbrella woman; the restaurant proprietor and his cook—the whole lot of them, whom he talked about as though he had always known them and whose idiosyncrasies he could list.

"What are you preparing for him for tomorrow?"

"Ragout of lamb. He likes to eat. Just now you seemed to be asking me what his chief interest is apart from work. It's probably food. And although he's sitting down all day and never gets any fresh air or exercise I've never seen a man with such an appetite."

"Before he met you had he any men friends?"

"I don't think so. He's never mentioned them."

"Did he live here then?"

"Yes. He kept house for himself. Except that once a week Madame Salazar would come and clean up properly. It may be because we don't need her any more that she's never liked me."

"Do the neighbors know?"

"What I used to do? No. At least they didn't until Frans was arrested. It was the reporters who brought that up."

"Are they cutting you?"

"Some of them. But Frans was so well liked that they're more inclined to be sorry for us."

This was true on the whole. If a count had been made in the street of those for them and those against, the "fors" would certainly have won.

But the residents of the neighborhood didn't want it to

be over too soon, any more than the newspaper readers did. The deeper the mystery, the more bitter the contest between the Police Judiciaire and Philippe Liotard, the more delighted people were.

"What did Alfonsi want?"

"He didn't have time to tell me. He'd just arrived when you came in. I don't like the way he comes in here as if it were a public place, with his hat on his head, saying *tu* to me and calling me by my first name. If Frans were here he'd have put him out long ago."

"Is he jealous?"

"He doesn't like familiarity."

"Does he love you?"

"I think so."

"Why?"

"I don't know. Perhaps because I love him."

He didn't smile. He hadn't kept his hat on, as Alfonsi had. He wasn't being rough and he wasn't wearing his cagey expression either.

There in the basement he really looked like a big man who is honestly try to understand.

"Obviously you're not going to say anything that may be used against him."

"Of course not. Anyhow I have nothing of the sort to say."

"And yet it's equally obvious that a man was killed in this basement."

"The experts say so, and I'm not educated enough to contradict them. In any case it wasn't Frans."

"It seems impossible that it could have happened without his knowing."

"I know what you're going to say, but I tell you again that he's innocent."

Maigret stood up, sighing. He was glad she hadn't offered him a drink, as so many people feel obliged to do in such circumstances.

"I'm trying to start afresh at the beginning," he admitted. "My intention in coming here was to go over the scene again inch by inch."

"You're not going to do that! They've turned everything upside down so many times!"

"I haven't the heart. I may come back. I expect I'll have some more questions to ask you."

"You know that I tell Frans everything on visiting day?"

"Yes. I understand you."

He started up the narrow stairs, and she followed him into the workshop, now almost dark, and opened the door for him. Both of them simultaneously noticed Alfonsi waiting at the corner of the street.

"Are you going to let him in?"

"I'm wondering. I'm sick and tired of it all."

"Would you like me to tell him to let you alone?"

"For tonight in any case."

"Good night."

She said good night too, and he walked heavily toward the former Vice Squad detective. When he came up with him, on the corner, two young reporters were watching them from the window of the Tabac des Vosges.

"Clear out."

"Why?"

"Never mind. Because she doesn't want you bothering her again tonight. See?"

"Why are you so hard on me?"

"Simply because I don't like your face."

And turning his back on him, he conformed to tradition by going into the Grand Turenne for a glass of beer.

# 3

# THE SHADY HOTEL IN THE RUE LEPIC

THE SUN WAS SHINING brightly, but there was a nip in the air that produced a cloud of vapor at your lips and froze your finger tips. All the same Maigret had decided to stand outside on the platform of the bus and he was alternately grunting and smiling in spite of himself as he read the morning paper.

He was early. It was barely eight-thirty by his watch when he entered the inspectors' office, at the very moment when Janvier, perched on a table, was trying to get down, hiding the newspaper from which he had been reading aloud.

There were five or six of them, mostly the young ones; they were waiting for Lucas to give them their day's orders. They avoided looking at the chief inspector, and some of them, casting a furtive glance at him, could hardly keep a straight face.

They had no way of knowing that the story had amused him just as much as it had them, and that it was simply to please them, because they expected it, that he was wearing his grouchy expression.

A headline was spread across three columns on the front page:

## MME. MAIGRET'S MISADVENTURE

The adventure encountered the previous day in the Place d'Anvers by the chief inspector's wife was recounted down to the last detail; and the only thing lacking was a photograph of Madame Maigret herself together with the little boy left on her hands in such cavalier fashion.

Maigret pushed open Lucas' door. He had read the story too and had good reason to take the matter more seriously.

"I hope you didn't think I was responsible for it? I was thunderstruck this morning when I opened the paper. Honestly, I didn't talk to a single reporter. Just after our conversation yesterday I called Lamballe of the Ninth Arrondissement and I had to tell him the story, but without mentioning your wife's name, when I asked him to try to find the taxi. By the way, he's just phoned to say that by sheer chance he's already found the driver. He's sending him over. The man will be here in a few minutes."

"Was there anyone in your office when you called Lamballe?"

"Probably. There's always somebody in here. And no doubt the door to the inspectors' office was open. But who? It frightens me to think that there might be a leak right here."

"I suspected it yesterday. There was a leak as far back as February 21, because when you went to the Rue de Turenne to search the bookbinder's premises Philippe Liotard had already been notified."

"Who by?"

"I don't know. It could only be somebody from here."

"That's why the suitcase had disappeared by the time I got there."

"More than likely."

"In that case why didn't they dispose of the blood-stained suit too?"

"Perhaps they didn't think of it, or else they thought we wouldn't find out what kind of stains they were. Perhaps they didn't have time."

"Do you want me to question the inspectors, Chief?"

"I'll take care of it."

Lucas had not finished going through his mail, which was stacked up on the long table he was using as a desk.

"Nothing interesting?"

"I don't know yet. I'll have to check. Several tips about the suitcase, of course. An anonymous letter states simply that it hasn't left the Rue de Turenne and that we must be blind not to find it. Another claims that the root of the matter is at Concarneau. A five-page letter, closely written, reveals with supporting arguments that the government itself fabricated the whole business out of nothing at all in order to divert attention from the cost of living."

Maigret went into his own office, took off his hat and coat, then, despite the mildness of the weather, filled to the brim the only coal stove still in existence at the Quai des Orfèvres: the one he had had such a hard time keeping possession of when central heating was installed.

Opening the inspectors' door a crack, he called in little Lapointe, who had just arrived.

"Sit down."

He closed the door again carefully, told the young man once more to sit down and walked around him once or twice, glancing at him curiously.

"You're ambitious, aren't you?"

"Yes, Chief Inspector. I'd like to have a career like yours. You might even call me presumptuous, I suppose."

"Are your parents well off?"

"No. My father's a bank clerk in Meulan and he had a hard time raising us decently—my sisters and myself."

"Are you in love?"

He did not blush or get embarrassed.

"No. Not yet. I still have time. I'm only twenty-four and I don't want to get married before I'm settled."

"Do you live by yourself in a furnished room?"

"Fortunately not. My youngest sister, Germaine, is in Paris too. She works for a publisher on the Left Bank. We share a place, and at night she has time to cook for us, and that's a saving."

"Has she a beau?"

"She's only eighteen."

"The first time you went to the Rue de Turenne did you come straight back here?"

Lapointe suddenly blushed, hesitated a moment before replying.

"No," he finally admitted. "I was so proud and happy at having discovered something that I treated myself to a taxi and went around to the Rue du Bac to tell Germaine about it."

"That's all, my boy. Thanks."

Lapointe, uneasy, worried, was reluctant to leave.

"Why did you ask me that?"

"I'm the one who asks the questions, aren't I? Later on maybe you'll get a chance to do some interrogating too. Were you in Sergeant Lucas' office yesterday when he telephoned the Ninth Arrondissement?"

"I was in the next office, and the door between them was open."

"What time did you talk to your sister?"

"How do you know I did?"

"Answer me."

"She gets off work at five. She waited for me, as she often does, at the Bar de la Grosse Horloge, and we had a drink together before going home."

"Were you with her all evening?"

"She went to the movies with a girl friend."

"Did you see her girl friend?"

"No. But I know her."

"That's all. You can go."

He would have liked to offer a bit more explanation, but someone came to tell the chief inspector that a taxi driver was asking to see him. This was a big, red-faced man of around fifty who must have driven a hackney carriage in his younger days and who, judging by his breath, had certainly swallowed several glasses of white wine for the good of his stomach before reporting.

"Inspector Lamballe told me to come and see you about the young lady."

"How did he find out that it was you who picked her up?"

"I'm usually parked in the Place Pigalle, and he came over for a word with me last night, the same way he had a word with all of us. It was me who picked her up."

"What time? Where?"

"It must have been about one o'clock. I was finishing my lunch at a restaurant in the Rue Lepic. My cab was outside. I saw a couple leaving the hotel opposite, and the woman immediately made a dash for my taxi. She seemed to be disappointed when she saw the flag was down. Since I'd got as far as my liqueur, I stood up and called across the street to her to wait."

"What was her companion like?"

"A fat little man, very well dressed. Looked like a foreigner. Between forty and fifty; I can't say exactly. I didn't look at him much. He was turned to face her and he was talking to her in a foreign language."

"What language?"

"I don't know. I come from Pantin and I've never been able to tell one lingo from another."

"What address did she give?"

"She was jumpy, impatient. She asked me to go through the Place d'Anvers first and slow down. She was looking out of the window.

"Then she said: 'Stop a minute and drive on again when I tell you.'

"She was beckoning to somebody. A motherly old soul was walking toward us with a little boy. The lady opened the door, pulled the kid in and ordered me to drive on."

"Didn't it look to you like a kidnaping?"

"No. Because she spoke to the lady. Not for long. Just a few words. And the lady seemed more relieved than anything else."

"Where did you take the mother and child?"

"First to the Porte de Neuilly. There she changed her mind and asked me to drive to the Gare Saint-Lazare."

"Did she get out there?"

"No. She stopped me in the Place Saint-Augustin. I got caught in a traffic jam there, and I saw her in my mirror hailing another cab, one of the Urbaine's, but I didn't have time to get its number."

"Did you try to?"

"Out of habit. She really was upset. And it was a bit queer, after taking me all the way to the Porte de Neuilly, to stop me on the Place Saint-Augustin just to get into another cab."

"Did she talk to the child on the way?"

"A sentence or two, to keep him quiet. Is there a reward?"

"There may be. I don't know yet."

"You see, I've wasted my morning."

Maigret handed him a bill and a few minutes later was pushing open the door of the director of the Police Judiciaire, where the daily briefing had begun. The department heads were there, grouped around the big mahogany desk, talking quietly about current cases.

"What about you, Maigret? And your Steuvels?"

From their smiles it was obvious that they had all read the morning's story. Once more, and again just to please them, he pretended to be disgruntled.

It was half past nine. The telephone rang; the director answered and handed the instrument to Maigret.

"Torrence wants to speak to you."

Torrence' voice at the other of the line was excited.

"Is that you, Chief? You haven't found the lady in the white hat? The Paris paper's just arrived, and I've read the story. Well, the description fits someone I'm on the track of here."

"Go on."

"Since there's no way of getting anything out of the fool of a postmistress here, who's pretending to have lost her memory, I started a search in the hotels and rooming houses, questioning garagemen and railway station employees."

"I know."

"The season hasn't started yet, and most of the people arriving at Concarneau are local residents or people who are more or less familiar, traveling salesmen and——"

"Make it short."

He was aware that conversation had been broken off all around him.

"I was thinking that if someone had come from Paris or somewhere else in order to send off the telegram——"

"Yes, yes. I get you."

"Well! There's a young lady in a blue suit and a white hat who arrived the very evening the telegram was sent off. She came in by the four o'clock train, and the message was handed in at a quarter to five."

"Did she have any luggage?"

"No. Wait. She didn't stop at the hotel. Do you know the Hôtel du Chien Jaune down by the pier? She had dinner there and sat around in a corner of the café until eleven o'clock. In other words, she left again on the eleven-forty train."

"Have you verified that?"

"I haven't had time yet, but I'm certain of it because

she left the café at exactly the right time and she asked for the railway timetable immediately after she'd had dinner."

"Didn't she speak to anyone?"

"Only to the waitress. She read the whole time, even while she was eating."

"Have you been able to find out what kind of book she was reading?"

"No. The waitress maintains that she had a foreign accent, but she doesn't know what it was. What shall I do?"

"Go back and see the postmistress, of course."

"And after that?"

"Call me or call Lucas if I'm not in the office. Then come back."

"All right, Chief. Do you think it's the same person too?"

When he hung up Maigret had a little spark of glee in his eye.

"Maybe Madame Maigret will be the one who puts us on the track," he said. "Will you excuse me, Chief? I have some urgent checking to do myself."

By chance Lapointe was still in the inspectors' office, visibly worried.

"You there, come with me!"

They took one of the cabs parked on the quay; and young Lapointe didn't feel any less worried, for it was the first time the chief inspector had taken him out with him like this.

"Corner of the Place Blanche and the Rue Lepic."

It was the time of day when in Montmartre and especially in the Rue Lepic carts were lined up along the sidewalks, piled high with vegetables and fruit fragrant with the smell of earth and springtime.

Maigret recognized on his left the little table d'hôte restaurant where the taxi driver had had lunch and, opposite, the Hôtel Beauséjour, the narrow doorway of which was visible between two stores, a delicatessen and a grocery.

> Rooms by the month, week or day. Running
> water. Central heating. Reasonable rates.

There was a glass door at the end of the hallway, then a staircase with a sign on the wall: *Office*. A hand drawn in black ink pointed upstairs.

"Anyone there?" he called.

The smell reminded him of the time when he was just about Lapointe's age and in the "Flophouse Squad" and used to spend his days going from one rooming house to another. It smelled of a mixture of dirty washing and sweat, unmade beds, slop pails and food being warmed up on spirit lamps.

A slatternly woman with red hair leaned over the banister.

"What is it?"

Then, all at once, realizing that it was the police, she snapped crossly:

"I'm coming."

She took her time upstairs, moving buckets and brooms; finally she appeared, buttoning her blouse over her protruding bosom. At closer range her hair proved to be almost white at the roots.

"What's the matter? They checked here only yesterday, and I have nothing but quiet tenants. You're not from the Flophouse Squad, are you?"

Without answering he described to her, so far as the taxi driver's testimony permitted, the companion of the lady with the white hat.

"Do you know him?"

"I may. I'm not sure. What's his name?"

"That's just what I'd like to know."

"Do you want to see my book?"

"First I want you to tell me whether you have a tenant who looks like him."

"Nobody except Monsieur Levine."

"Who's he?"

"I don't know. A very decent man, anyhow, who paid for a week in advance."

"Is he still here?"

"No, he left yesterday."

"Alone?"

"With the little boy, of course."

"And the lady?"

"Do you mean the nursemaid?"

"Just a minute. Let's begin at the beginning so as to save time."

"That'll be fine because I haven't any to spare. What's Monsieur Levine done?"

"Just answer my questions, will you? When did he arrive?"

"Four days ago. You can check in my book. I told him I didn't have a vacant room, and it was true. He insisted. I asked him how long for, and he told me he'd pay for a week in advance."

"How could you accommodate him if you had no room?"

Maigret knew the answer but he wanted to make her say it. In this kind of hotel the second-floor rooms are generally reserved for transient couples coming in for a few minutes or an hour.

"There are always the rooms for the 'casual trade,'" she replied, using the traditional term.

"Was the child with him?"

"Not at the time. He went to fetch him and came back with him an hour later. I asked him how he was going to manage with such a young child, and he told me that a nursemaid he knew would take care of him most of the day."

"Did he show you his passport or his identity card?"

According to regulations, she ought to have asked for these documents, but she obviously hadn't complied.

"He filled out his slip himself. I saw at once that he was a respectable man. Are you going to make trouble for me just for that?"

"Not necessarily. How was the nursemaid dressed?"

"In a blue suit."

"With a white hat?"

"Yes. She would come in the morning and give the kid his bath and then take him out."

"And Monsieur Levine?"

"He would hang around in his room until eleven or twelve o'clock. I think he went back to bed. Then he would go out, and I wouldn't see him again all day."

"And the child?"

"Nor him either. Not much before seven o'clock at night. It was the lady who would bring him back and put him to bed. She would lie down on the bed fully dressed while she waited for Monsieur Levine to come home."

"What time did he come in?"

"Not before one."

"Would she leave then?"

"Yes."

"You don't know where she lived?"

"No. I only know that she took a cab when she left, because I saw her."

"Was she intimate with your tenant?"

"Do you mean did they sleep together? I'm not sure. From certain indications I think they did sometimes. They have a right to, haven't they?"

"What nationality did Monsieur Levine write down on his slip?"

"French. He told me he'd been in France a long time and was naturalized."

"Where did he come from?"

"I don't remember. Your man from the Flophouse Squad

called for the slips yesterday, as he does every Tuesday. From Bordeaux, if I'm not mistaken."

"What happened yesterday at noon?"

"I don't know about noon."

"During the morning then?"

"Someone called and asked for him about ten o'clock. The lady and the kid had been gone quite a while."

"Who called?"

"I didn't ask him his name. An ordinary little man, not very well dressed, a bit shabby."

"French?"

"Certainly. I told him the room number."

"He'd never been here before?"

"No one had ever called except the nursemaid."

"Did he have a southern accent?"

"More like a Paris accent. You know, the kind of man who stops you in the street trying to sell you fancy postcards or take you Lord knows where."

"Did he stay long?"

"Well, he stayed alone while Monsieur Levine was checking out."

"With his luggage?"

"How did you know? I was amazed to see him carrying his luggage out."

"Did he have much?"

"Four suitcases."

"Brown ones?"

"Nearly all suitcases are brown, aren't they? Anyhow these were good quality, and at least two of them were solid leather."

"What did he say to you?"

"That he had to go away unexpectedly; that he'd be leaving Paris that day but he'd be back in a little while for the child's things."

"How much later did he come back?"

"About an hour. The lady was with him."

"Weren't you surprised not to see the little boy?"

"So you know about that too?"

She was growing more cautious because she was beginning to suspect that the matter was of some importance and that the police knew more about it than Maigret wanted to tell her.

"All three of them stayed in the room quite a time and they were talking pretty loud."

"As if they were quarreling?"

"As if they were arguing at least."

"In French?"

"No."

"Did the Frenchman take part in the conversation?"

"Not much. Anyhow he went out first, and I didn't see him again. Then later Monsieur Levine and the lady left. As they passed me on their way out they thanked me and told me they expected to be back in a few days."

"Didn't it seem queer to you?"

"If you'd kept a hotel like this one for eighteen years, nothing would seem queer to you."

"Did you clean up their room yourself afterward?"

"I helped the maid."

"Did you find anything?"

"Cigarette ends all over the place. He smoked more than fifty a day. American cigarettes. And newspapers. He bought just about all the papers published in Paris."

"No foreign newspapers?"

"No. I thought of that."

"So you were curious?"

"You always like to know what's going on."

"What else?"

"The usual mess—a broken comb, torn underclothing . . ."

"Any initials?"

"No. The kid's underclothing."

"Good quality?"

"Pretty good, yes. Better than I'm used to seeing around here."

"I'll be back to see you again."

"What for?"

"Because some details that escape you at present will certainly come back to you when you think it over. You've always been on good terms with the police, haven't you? The Flophouse Squad doesn't bother you too much, does it?"

"I get you. But I don't know any more."

"Good morning."

He and Lapointe were back on the sunny sidewalk in the midst of the bustle.

"A little drink?" suggested the chief inspector.

"I don't drink."

"You're quite right. Have you thought things over in the meantime?"

The young man realized that he wasn't talking about what they had just found out at the hotel.

"Yes."

"Well?"

"I'll speak to her tonight."

"Do you know who it is?"

"I have a friend who's a reporter on the same paper that printed that story this morning, but I didn't see him yesterday. Anyway I never talk to him about what goes on at the Quai. In fact he often teases me about that."

"Does your sister know him?"

"Yes. I didn't think they were going around together. If I tell my father he'll make her come back to Meulan."

"What's the reporter's name?"

"Bizard. Antoine Bizard. He's on his own in Paris too. His family lives in Corrèze. He's two years younger than I, and some of his articles carry his own by-line already."

"Do you meet your sister at lunchtime?"

"It depends. When I'm free and not too far from the

Rue du Bac I go to lunch with her in a little restaurant near her office."

"Go and meet her today. Tell her what we found out this morning."

"You really want me to?"

"Yes."

"What if she passes this on too?"

"She will."

"Is that what you want her to do?"

"Go ahead. But be sure to be nice to her. Don't let it look as if you're suspicious of her."

"But I can't have her going out with a young man whatever happens. My father told me to be sure——"

"Go on."

Maigret walked down the Rue Notre-Dame-de-Lorette just for the pleasure of walking and took a taxi only at the Faubourg Montmartre after stopping by a bar for a glass of beer.

"Quai des Orfèvres."

Then he changed his mind; rapped on the glass.

"No. Go through the Rue de Turenne."

He saw Steuvels' shop with its door shut, as it was every morning now, for Fernande must have been on her way to the Santé with her stack of casseroles.

"Stop a minute."

Janvier was at the bar of the Grand Turenne and, recognizing him, gave him a wink. What was the latest item Lucas had told him to check? He was deep in conversation with the shoemaker and two plasterers in white overalls, and the milky tint of their Pernods was recognizable from quite a distance.

"Turn left. Drive through the Place des Vosges and the Rue de Birague."

This meant passing the Tabac des Vosges, where Alfonsi was sitting alone at a little table near the window.

"Are you getting out?"

"Yes. Wait for me a minute."

It was the Grand Turenne he entered, after all, to have a word with Janvier.

"Alfonsi's across the street. Have you seen any newspapermen over there this morning?"

"Two or three."

"Know them?"

"Not all of them."

"Have you got much more to do?"

"Nothing much. And if you have anything else for me I'm free. I just wanted to talk to the shoemaker."

They were a good distance away from the group and were speaking in lowered voices.

"Something that occurred to me just now, after I read the story. The old boy talks far too much, you know. He's determined to be somebody and he'd make things up if necessary. Besides, every time he finds something to tell it means a few drinks for him. Seeing that he lives right opposite Steuvels' studio and works in his window too, I asked him whether any women ever came to see the bookbinder."

"What did he say?"

"Not much. He remembers one old lady in particular; she must be rich and she comes in a limousine with a chauffeur in livery who carries her books in. Also, about a month ago, a very elegant young lady in a mink coat. Wait! I made a point of finding out if she only called once. He says not! She came again a couple of weeks ago, in a blue suit with a white hat. It was a day when the weather was beautiful, and the paper apparently carried an article on the chestnut tree in the Boulevard Saint-Germain."

"We can trace that."

"That's what I thought."

"So she went down to the basement?"

"No. But I'm a bit suspicious. He's read the article too, that's obvious, and it's entirely possible that he's making it all up just to get some attention. What do you want me to do?"

"Keep an eye on Alfonsi. Don't let him out of your sight all day. You're to make a list of the people he speaks to."

"He's not supposed to know I'm tailing him?"

"It doesn't matter much if he does."

"What if he speaks to me?"

"Answer him."

Maigret went out with the smell of Pernod in his nostrils, and his cab dropped him at the Quai, where he found Lucas in the middle of a lunch consisting of sandwiches. There were two glasses of beer on the desk, and the chief inspector took one of them without compunction.

"Torrence has just phoned. The postmistress thinks she remembers a customer with a white hat, but she can't swear she's the one who handed in the telegram. According to Torrence, even if she were dead sure she wouldn't say so."

"Is he coming back?"

"He'll be in Paris tonight."

"Call the Urbaine Taxi Company, will you? There's another cab to be traced, possibly two."

Had Madame Maigret, who had another appointment with her dentist, left early, as she had the previous times, in order to spend a few minutes on the bench in the Place d'Anvers park?

Maigret didn't go home to the Boulevard Richard-Lenoir for lunch. Lucas' sandwiches looked tempting, and he had some sent up from the Brasserie Dauphine for himself.

This was usually a good sign.

# 4

## FERNANDE'S ADVENTURE

YOUNG LAPOINTE, red-eyed and rumpled like somebody who has slept on a bench in a third-class waiting room, gave Maigret a look of such distress when the latter entered the inspectors' office that the chief inspector immediately took him into his own room.

"The whole business of the Hôtel Beauséjour's in the paper," said the young man lugubriously.

"That's good! I'd have been disappointed if it hadn't been."

Then Maigret deliberately began to talk to him as he would have talked to one of the old hands, to Lucas or Torrence, for instance.

"There are some people we know practically nothing about, not even whether they've really played any part in the case. There's a woman, a little boy, a rather stout man and another man who looks a bit seedy. Are they still in Paris? We don't know. If they are, they've probably split up. The woman has only to take off her white hat and get rid of the child and we can't recognize her any more. Do you follow me?"

"Yes, Chief Inspector. I think I understand. But all the

57

same I don't like to think that my sister saw that fellow again last night."

"You can worry about your sister later. Right now you're working with me. This morning's newspaper story has alarmed them. There are two possibilities: either they'll stay holed up, if they have anywhere to hole up, or they'll look for a safer hiding place. In any case our only chance is for them to do something to give themselves away."

"Yes."

Just at that point Judge Dossin telephoned to express his surprise at the newspaper's disclosures, and Maigret began to sum up the position again.

"Everybody's been alerted, Monsieur le Juge: the stations, the airports, the cheap hotels, the highway police. Moers up in Criminal Records is busy looking for photos which might correspond to our customers. They're questioning taxi drivers and, in case our boys have a car, garagemen."

"Do you think this has some connection with the Steuvels case?"

"It's a lead—after so many that haven't got us anywhere."

"I'm having Steuvels brought up this morning at eleven. His lawyer will be here, as usual, because he won't let me exchange two words with him except in his presence."

"Would you permit me to come up for a minute during your interrogation?"

"Liotard will protest, but come up anyway. It won't look as if we'd planned it."

The curious thing was that Maigret had never met this Liotard, who had become, in the press at all events, something like his personal enemy.

This morning all the papers again carried the young lawyer's comments on the latest angles of the case.

Maigret is a policeman of the old school, of the

period when the gentlemen of the Quai des Orfèvres could, if they chose, give a man the third degree until weariness drove him to admit everything, keep him in their hands for weeks, pry shamelessly into people's private lives—a period when any kind of trick was considered legitimate.

He is the only person who doesn't realize that to an informed public, tricks like these constitute nothing but monkey business.

What is it all about, really?

He has let himself be fooled by an anonymous letter, the work of a prankster. He has had an honest man locked up and has been incapable ever since of pinning any serious charge on him.

He won't give up. Rather than admit defeat, he is trying to gain time, playing to the gallery, calling in Madame Maigret to the rescue, serving up to the public slices of cheap fiction.

Believe me, gentlemen, Maigret is out of date.

"Stay here with me, my boy," the chief inspector was saying to young Lapointe. "Only tonight, before you go home, ask me what you may tell your sister, won't you?"

"I'll never tell her anything again."

"You tell her what I ask you to tell her."

And from then on Lapointe acted as his aide-de-camp. And that really meant something, for the Police Judiciaire was becoming more and more like a military headquarters.

The office of Lucas, The Great Turenne, represented the command post, to which runners made their way from all floors. Downstairs, in the Flophouse Squad, several men were busy going through hotel registrations in search of a Levine or anybody else who might be connected with the trio and the child.

The previous night, in most cheap hotels, the guests had had the unpleasant surprise of being awakened by the police, who had examined their identity documents; this had resulted in some fifty men and women whose papers were not in order spending the rest of the night in the lockup at headquarters, where they were now lining up outside the Criminal Identification Department.

In the railway station travelers were being scrutinized without their knowing it, and two hours after the papers came out the telephone calls began, soon becoming so numerous that Lucas had to detail an inspector to this job.

People had seen the little boy all over the place, in the most widely separated parts of Paris and the suburbs; some of them had seen him with the lady in the white hat, some of them with the gentleman with the foreign accent.

Pedestrians would suddenly rush up to a patrolman: "Hurry! The child's at the corner of the street."

Everything was checked; everything had to be checked if no chance were to be overlooked. Three detectives had gone out first thing to interrogate garagemen.

And all night long the men of the Night Life Squad had been on the job too. Hadn't the proprietress of the Beauséjour said that her tenant hardly ever came home before one o'clock?

Their task was to find out if he was a regular patron of night clubs, to question bartenders and bar girls.

Maigret, after sitting through the daily briefing in the chief's office, was prowling about the building, with Lapointe at his side most of the time, going down to the Flophouse Squad, up to Moers in Criminal Records, taking a telephone call here, a statement there.

It was just after ten o'clock when a driver from the Urbaine Company phoned. He hadn't called earlier because he had made a trip out of town, to Dreux, with an old invalid lady who did not want to go by train.

It was he who had picked up the young lady and the little boy in the Place Saint-Augustin; he remembered it perfectly well.

"Where did you take them to?"

"The corner of the Rue Montmartre and the Grands Boulevards."

"Was there anyone waiting for them?"

"I didn't notice anyone."

"You don't know which way they went?"

"I lost sight of them right away in the crowd."

There were several hotels in the vicinity.

"Call the Flophouse Squad again," said Maigret to Lapointe. "Tell them to go over the sector around the Carrefour Montmartre again with a fine comb. Do you realize now that if they don't lose their heads, if they don't budge, we haven't the remotest chance of finding them?"

Torrence, back from Concarneau, had gone for a stroll down the Rue de Turenne, to get back into the feel of it, as he said.

As for Janvier, he had sent in a report on his shadowing assignment and was still on Alfonsi's tail.

The latter had joined Philippe Liotard the night before in a restaurant on the Rue Richelieu, where they had had a good dinner, chatting quietly. Two women had joined them later, neither of whom bore any resemblance to the young lady in the white hat. One was the lawyer's secretary, a big blonde with the look of a movie starlet. The other had left with Alfonsi.

They had both gone to the movies, near the Opéra, then to a night club on the Rue Blanche where they had remained until two o'clock in the morning.

After which the ex-detective had taken his companion to the hotel where he lived in the Rue de Douai.

Janvier had taken a room at the same hotel. He had just phoned:

"They're not up yet. I'm waiting."

A little before eleven o'clock Lapointe, following Maigret, was introduced to a region of the Quai des Orfèvres which was unknown to him, on the ground floor. They went down a long deserted corridor, the windows of which overlooked the yard, and, reaching a corner, Maigret made a sign to the young man to keep quiet.

A patrol wagon, passing through the entrance gate to headquarters, was entering the yard. Three or four policemen were waiting, smoking cigarettes. Two others got out of the paddy wagon, from which they unloaded first a great brute of a man with a low forehead and handcuffs on his wrists. Maigret didn't know him. This one hadn't crossed his path.

Next came a fragile-looking old lady who might have been the chair custodian in a church, but whom he had arrested at least twenty times as a pickpocket. She followed her policeman like an old-timer, trotting along behind him with little steps in her extra-wide skirts, taking the right turnings for the examining magistrates' offices without being told.

The sun was bright, the air steely blue in the patches of shade, with whiffs of springtime and a few newly hatched flies buzzing.

Frans Steuvels' red head appeared, bare of hat or cap; his suit was rather crushed. He stopped, as though surprised by the sun, and one guessed that his eyes were half closing behind his thick glasses.

He had been handcuffed, just like the brute—a regulation strictly enforced since several prisoners had escaped from this very yard, the latest of them via the corridors of the Palais de Justice.

With his hunched back and his flabby figure, Steuvels was typical of those intellectual craftsmen who read everything that comes their way and have no consuming interest outside their work.

One of the guards handed him a lighted cigarette, and he thanked him, took a few drags on it with satisfaction, filling his lungs with air and tobacco.

He must have been easy to handle, because they were

treating him kindly; they gave him time to stretch his legs before taking him over to the building; and he for his part seemed not to bear his guards any ill will, showed no rancor, no hysteria.

There was a tiny bit of truth in Maître Liotard's interview. Normally Maigret himself would have completed the inquiry before turning the man over to the prosecuting magistrate.

If it had not been for the lawyer, who had appeared on the scene as soon as the first interrogation was over, Maigret would have seen Steuvels several more times, which would have given him a chance to study him.

He scarcely knew him, having been alone with the bookbinder for only ten or twelve hours, at a time when he still knew nothing about him or about the case.

Rarely had he been confronted with a prisoner so calm, so much in control of himself, and there had been no indication that this was an assumed attitude.

Steuvels had waited for the questions, head down, with an air of trying to understand, and he had watched Maigret as he would have watched a lecturer developing complicated ideas.

Then he had taken time to think, speaking in a gentle, rather faint voice, in carefully chosen phrases which, however, held no affectation.

He had not become impatient like most prisoners, and when the same question had come up for the twentieth time he had answered in the same terms, with remarkable equanimity.

Maigret would have liked to get to know him better, but for the last three weeks the man hadn't belonged to him any more but to Dossin, who had him brought up, with his lawyer, on an average of twice a week.

Fundamentally Steuvels must have been a shy man. The strangest thing was that the judge was a shy man too. Noticing the initial G. before his name, the chief inspector had once made so bold as to ask him his first name, and the distinguished magistrate had blushed.

"Don't tell anyone or they'll start calling me the Angel again, as my fellow students did at school and later in law school too. My first name is Gabriel!"

"Come on now," Maigret was saying to Lapointe. "I want you to go and sit in my office and take all messages while you're waiting for me."

He did not go upstairs right away but wandered about the corridors a bit, his pipe between his teeth, his hands in his pockets, like a man who feels at home, shaking a hand here, another one there.

When he felt sure that the interrogation was under way he went up to the magistrates' block and knocked at Dossin's door.

"May I?"

"Come in, Chief Inspector."

A man had risen to his feet, small and slim, very slim, too deliberately well dressed, whom Maigret instantly recognized from his photographs in the papers. He was young and put on a pompous manner in order to look older, affecting a self-assurance which did not match his age.

Quite handsome, with a sallow complexion and black hair, he had long nostrils which quivered from time to time, and he stared people in the eye as though determined to make them look away.

"Monsieur Maigret, I suppose."

"Yes, indeed, Maître Liotard."

"If you're looking for me, I'll be glad to see you after the interview."

Frans Steuvels, who had remained seated, facing the judge, was waiting. He had merely glanced at the chief inspector, then at the police stenographer at the end of the desk, who still had his pen in his hand.

"I'm not looking for you particularly. I'm looking for a chair, believe it or not."

He picked one up by its back and straddled it, still smoking his pipe.

"Do you intend to stay here?"

"Unless Monsieur le Juge asks me to leave."

"Do stay, Maigret."

"I protest. If the interview is going to be conducted in these circumstances, I object strenuously on the grounds that the presence of a member of the police in this office obviously tends to influence my client."

Maigret refrained from muttering: "Get it off your chest, my boy."

And he watched the young lawyer with an ironical expression. The latter obviously didn't believe a word he was saying. It was part of his system. In every interview so far he had precipitated incidents, for the most futile or extravagant reasons.

"There's no regulation to prevent an officer of the Police Judiciaire from being present at an interrogation. So if you don't mind we'll go on where we left off."

All the same Dossin was influenced by Maigret's presence and he took a little while to find his place in his notes.

"I was asking you, Steuvels, if you are in the habit of buying your clothes ready-made or if you have a tailor."

"It depends," the prisoner replied after reflecting.

"On what?"

"I hardly bother about clothes at all. When I need a suit I sometimes get it ready-made, but I've also had them made for me."

"By which tailor?"

"I had a suit made several years ago by a neighbor, a Polish Jew, who has since disappeared. I think he went to America."

"Was it a blue suit?"

"No. It was gray."

"How long did you wear it?"

"Two or three years. I forget."

"And your blue suit?"

"It must be ten years since I bought a blue suit."

"But the neighbors saw you dressed in blue not so long ago."

"They must have confused my suit with my overcoat."

It was true that a navy-blue overcoat had been found in the apartment.

"When did you buy this overcoat?"

"Last winter."

"Isn't it unlikely that you would buy a blue overcoat if your only suit was brown? The two colors don't match particularly well."

"I'm not so stylish."

All this time Maître Liotard was staring at Maigret with a look of defiance so intense that he seemed to be trying to hypnotize him. Then, just as he would have done in court to impress the jury, he shrugged his shoulders, a sarcastic smile on his lips.

"Why don't you admit that the suit found in the closet belongs to you?"

"Because it doesn't."

"How do you account for someone having managed to place it there, seeing that you practically never leave your house and your room can be reached only by going through the workshop?"

"I don't explain it."

"Let's be reasonable, Monsieur Steuvels. I'm not trying to trap you. This is the third time at least that we've approached this subject. According to you, somebody entered your home, unknown to you, to place two human teeth in the ashes of your furnace. Note that this person chose the day when your wife was absent and that in order to make sure she would be absent he had to go to Concarneau—or send an accomplice—to dispatch a telegram about her mother's illness. Wait! That's not all.

"Not only were you alone at home, which is hardly ever

the case, but furthermore, that day and the following one, you had such a big fire going in the furnace that it took you seven trips to carry the ashes out to the garbage cans.

"On this point we have the evidence of your concierge, Madame Salazar, who has no reason to lie and who is in a good position, in her apartment, to keep an eye on the comings and goings of her tenants. On Sunday morning you made five trips, each time with a big bucket full of ashes.

"She thought you had been doing some spring cleaning and burning old papers.

"We have more evidence, from Mademoiselle Béguin who lives on the top floor and who states that your chimney smoked incessantly all day Sunday. Black smoke, she specifies. At one point she opened her window and noticed an unpleasant smell."

"Is it not a fact that Old Lady Béguin, who is sixty-eight, is generally regarded as not quite all there?" the lawyer interrupted, crushing out his cigarette in the ash tray and taking another from a silver case. "May I also point out that for four days, as the weather reports for February 15, 16, 17 and 18 prove, the temperature in Paris and its surroundings was abnormally low?"

"That doesn't explain the teeth. Neither does it explain the presence of the blue suit in the closet or the bloodstains on it."

"You're making the charge and it's up to you to prove it. But you're not even able to prove that the suit actually belongs to my client."

"Might I ask a question, Monsieur le Juge?"

The magistrate turned to the lawyer, who had no time to protest, since Maigret, turning to face the man from Flanders, was already continuing:

"When did you first hear of Maître Philippe Liotard?"

The lawyer stood up to make a retort, and Maigret, unperturbed, went on:

"When I finished questioning you on the night of your

arrest, or rather in the early hours of the morning, and asked you if you wanted the services of a lawyer, you answered affirmatively and nominated Maître Liotard."

"The prisoner has a perfect right to choose any lawer he likes, and if this question is asked again I shall be obliged to bring the matter up before the Bar Association."

"Go ahead. Go ahead and bring it. It's you I'm talking to, Steuvels. You haven't answered me.

"It wouldn't have been at all surprising if you had mentioned the name of a famous counsel or lawyer but that's not the case.

"In my office you didn't consult any directory; you didn't ask anybody any questions.

"Maître Liotard doesn't live in your neighborhood. I believe that until three weeks ago his name had never appeared in the paper."

"I protest."

"Protest all you like. As for you, Steuvels, tell me whether, on the morning of the twenty-first, before my detective's visit, you had ever heard of Maître Liotard. If you had, tell me when and where."

"Don't answer."

The man from Flanders hesitated, his back hunched, watching Maigret through his thick glasses.

"You refuse to answer? All right. I'll ask you something else. Did you receive a telephone call on that same day, the twenty-first, during the afternoon, about Maître Liotard?"

Frans Steuvels was still hesitating.

"Or if you prefer it, did you call anybody? I'm going to take you back to the atmosphere of that day, which had begun just like any other day. The sun was shining, and it was very mild, so you hadn't started the furnace. You were at work, facing your window, when my detective appeared and asked to inspect your premises on some pretext or other."

"So you admit that!" interrupted Liotard.

"I admit it, Maître. It's not you I'm interrogating.

"You immediately realized that the police had their eye on you, Steuvels.

"At that time there was a brown suitcase in your workshop which was gone that evening when Inspector Lucas came with a search warrant.

"Who phoned you? Whom did you warn? Who came to see you between the visits of Lapointe and Lucas?

"I've had a check made of the list of people you call frequently, whose numbers you've written down on a pad. I checked your telephone directory myself. Liotard's name does not appear among those of your clients either.

"And yet he came to see you that day. Did you send for him or did someone you know send him to you?"

"I forbid you to answer."

But the man from Flanders made a gesture of impatience.

"He came on his own."

"You are referring to Maître Liotard, aren't you?"

Then the bookbinder looked at each of the men around him, and his eyes shone as if he took a certain personal delight in putting his lawyer in an embarrassing position.

"Yes. Maître Liotard."

The latter turned to the police stenographer, who was writing.

"You have no right to put these answers on record. They have nothing to do with the case. I did, in fact, go to see Steuvels, whose reputation was known to me, to ask him if he could do a binding job for me. Is that so?"

"That's so."

Why in the world was a malicious little spark dancing in the bright pupils of Steuvels' eyes?

"It was actually about a bookplate with the family coat of arms—oh, yes, Monsieur Maigret, my grandfather was known as the Comte de Liotard and voluntarily stopped using his title when he lost all his money. So I wanted a family coat of arms and came to Steuvels, whom I knew to be the best bookbinder in Paris, though I had been told he was terribly busy."

"You didn't talk to him about anything except your coat of arms?"

"Excuse me, it seems to me that you are now interrogating me. Monsieur le Juge, this is your office, and I don't wish to be called to account by a member of the police. Even when it was my client who was concerned I had serious objections. But for a member of the Bar . . ."

"Have you any other questions to put to Steuvels, Chief Inspector?"

"No more, thank you."

It was funny. It still seemed to him that the bookbinder was not annoyed at what had happened and that he was looking at him with new-found liking.

As for the lawyer, he was sitting down again, picking up a file in which he pretended to be absorbed.

"You'll find me any time you want me, Maître Liotard. Do you know my office? The next to the last on the left, at the end of the corridor."

He smiled at Judge Dossin, who was not feeling very comfortable, and walked toward the little door that connects the Police Judiciaire with the Palais de Justice.

The place was more of a beehive than ever. Telephones in use behind every door, people waiting in every corner, inspectors rushing up and down the corridors.

"I think there's someone waiting for you in your office, Chief Inspector."

When he pushed the door open he found Fernande alone with Lapointe, who, sitting in Maigret's place, was listening to her and taking notes. He stood up in some confusion. The bookbinder's wife was wearing a beige gabardine raincoat and a hat of the same stuff, quite without style.

"How is he?" she asked. "Have you just seen him? Is he still up there?"

"He's getting on very well. He admits that Liotard called at the studio on the afternoon of the twenty-first."

"A more disturbing thing has just happened," she said. "Please, please take what I'm about to tell you seriously. This morning I left the Rue de Turenne as usual to take his dinner to the Santé. You know the little enamel casseroles I put it in?

"I took the métro at the Saint-Paul station and changed at the Châtelet. I'd bought a paper on the way because I hadn't had time to read one.

"There was a seat near the door. I sat down in it and began the article—you know the one I mean.

"I had put the stack of casseroles on the floor beside me and I could feel the heat from them against my leg.

"There must have been a train due because a few stations before Montparnasse a lot of people got into the car, and a good many of them had suitcases.

"I was busy reading and not paying attention to what was going on around me when I got the impression that someone was touching my casseroles.

"I just had time to see a hand trying to put the metal handle back in position.

"I stood up, turning to face the person next to me. We were pulling into Montparnasse, where I had to change. Nearly everybody was getting out.

"I don't know how he did it, but he managed to upset the whole thing and make his way out on to the platform before I could see him full face.

"The food spilled all over the place. I've brought you the casseroles, which are practically empty, except for the bottom one.

"Look at them for yourself. A strip of metal with a handle on top holds them together. It can't open by itself.

I'm sure somebody was following me and tried to slip some poison into the food meant for Frans."

"Take it to the lab," said Maigret to Lapointe.

"They may not find anything, because of course it was the top one they tried to put the poison in and it's empty. Can't you believe me just the same, Chief Inspector? You must have realized that I've been honest with you."

"Always?"

"As far as possible. This time Frans's life is at stake. They're trying to get rid of him, and those dirty crooks wanted to use me without my knowing it."

Her bitterness was brimming over.

"If only I hadn't been so absorbed in my paper I might have had a good look at the man. The only thing I know is that he was wearing a raincoat just about the color of mine, and that his black shoes were worn."

"Young?"

"Not very. Not old either. Middle-aged. Or rather a man of no particular age, if you know what I mean. There was a stain near the shoulder of his raincoat. I noticed it while he was getting away."

"Tall? Slender?"

"Rather small. Average height at the most. Looked like a rat if you want my opinion."

"And you're sure you've never seen him before?"

She thought for a moment.

"No. He doesn't suggest anything."

Then, changing her mind:

"Now it's coming back to me. I was just reading the piece about the lady with the little boy at the Hôtel Beauséjour. He reminded me of one of those two men, the one the proprietress said looked like the type that sells fancy postcards. You're not laughing at me, are you?"

"No."

"You don't think I'm making it all up?"

"No."

"Do you think they were trying to kill him?"

"Possibly."

"What are you going to do?"

"I don't know yet."

Lapointe was coming back to say that the laboratory could not let them have a report for several hours.

"Do you think he'd better stick to prison food?"

"It would be safer."

"He'll be wondering why I haven't sent him his meal. I won't see him for two days, at visiting time."

She wasn't crying or making a fuss, but her dull eyes, deeply ringed, were full of anxiety and distress.

"Come with me."

He winked at Lapointe, led her downstairs, through corridors which became more and more deserted the farther they went. With some trouble he opened a little window overlooking the yard, where a patrol wagon was waiting.

"He'll be down in a minute. Will you excuse me? There's something I must attend to upstairs. . . ."

He was making a gesture toward the upper floor.

Incredulously she watched him, then took hold of the bars with both hands, trying to see as far as possible in the direction from which Steuvels was going to emerge.

# 5

## SOMETHING ABOUT A HAT

IT WAS RESTFUL, after leaving the office where doors
banged incessantly behind inspectors and where all the
telephones were ringing simultaneously, to make one's way,
via a permanently deserted staircase, up to the top floor of
the Palais de Justice, where the laboratories and records
were located.

It was already nearly dark, and in the badly lighted
stair well, which was like some secret staircase in a castle,
Maigret was preceded by his own gigantic shadow.

In a corner under the mansard roof Moers, a green eye-
shade on his forehead, his thick spectacles before his eyes,
was working under a lamp which he could move closer to
or farther away from his work by pulling a wire.

This man had not been to the Rue de Turenne to question the residents or to drink Pernods and white wine in
one of the three bars. He had never shadowed anyone in
the street or spent the night in some hiding place outside
a closed door.

He never got upset or nervous, yet quite likely tomorrow
morning would find him still hunched over his desk. Once
he had even spent three consecutive days and nights at it.

Maigret, without saying a word, picked up a cane-

74

bottomed chair, sat down near the inspector and lighted his pipe, on which he was puffing gently. Hearing a rhythmic sound on a skylight above his head, he realized that the weather had changed and it had begun to rain.

"Look at these, Chief," Moers was saying, handing him, like a deck of cards, a stack of photographs.

It was a magnificent job he had turned out, all by himself in his hideaway. From the vague specifications that he had been given he had somehow brought to life and endowed with personality three people of whom almost nothing was known: the fat, dark foreigner with the elegant clothes, the young woman with the white hat, and finally the accomplice who "looked like a man who sells fancy postcards."

To achieve this he had at his disposal hundreds of thousands of record cards, but he was certainly the only person who carried in his head sufficient knowledge of the data contained in them to be capable of the job he had just patiently turned out.

The first batch, which Maigret was examining, contained about fifty photographs of stout, well-groomed men, Greek or Levantine in type, with sleek hair and rings on their fingers.

"I'm not too pleased with those," sighed Moers, as if he was faced with selecting the ideal cast for a film. "But you can give them a try anyhow. As far as I'm concerned, I like these better."

There were only about fifteen photos in the second batch, and every one of them made one feel like applauding because they bore so close a resemblance to one's mental picture of the person described by the proprietress of the Beauséjour.

Turning them over, Maigret learned the profession of the subjects. Two or three were race-track tipsters. There was a pickpocket who was especially familiar to him because he had personally arrested him in a bus, and an individual who hung around outside big hotels touting for certain specialized establishments.

A satisfied little spark was dancing in Moers's eyes.

"It's amusing, isn't it? I've hardly got anything on the woman, because our photos never show hats. But I'll keep at it anyhow."

Maigret, who had slipped the photographs into his pocket, stayed a few minutes longer just because he felt like it, then, with a sigh, went on to the laboratory next door, where they were still working on the food in Fernande's casseroles.

They hadn't found anything. Either the story was a complete fabrication for some purpose which he couldn't guess, or there hadn't been time to introduce the poison, or else it had been in the portion that had all been spilled in the métro car.

Maigret avoided going back through the Police Judiciaire offices and came out into the rain on the Quai des Orfèvres, turned up his coat collar, walked toward the Pont Saint-Michel and had to hail about ten cabs before one stopped.

"Place Blanche. Corner of the Rue Lepic."

He felt out of sorts, dissatisfied with himself and with the way the case was going. He was particularly resentful of Philippe Liotard, who had forced him to abandon his usual methods and mobilize all departments right at the start.

Now too many people whom he couldn't control personally were mixed up in the case, which seemed to be getting more and more complicated all by itself; new characters were popping up about whom he knew almost nothing and whose roles he couldn't even guess at.

On two occasions he had been tempted to go back to the very beginning of the inquiry, on his own, slowly, deliberately, following his favorite method, but this was no longer possible; the machine was running, and there was no longer any way to stop it.

He would have liked, for instance, to question the concierge, the shoemaker across the street, the old maid on the fifth floor. But what was the use? Everybody had questioned them by now—inspectors, journalists, amateur detectives, people in the street. Their statements had been published in the papers, and they couldn't go back on them now. It was like a trail which has been heedlessly trampled on by fifty people.

"Do you think the bookbinder committed murder, Monsieur Maigret?"

It was the driver, who had recognized him and was questioning him as if they were on familiar terms.

"I don't know."

"If I were you I'd pay particular attention to the little boy. That seems to be the best lead, and I'm not saying that just because I have a kid his age."

Even the taxi drivers were getting into it! He got out at the corner of the Rue Lepic and went into the bar on the corner for a drink. The rain was dripping in big drops from the awning around the terrace, where a few women were sitting as rigid as waxworks. He knew most of them. Some of them probably took their clients to the Hôtel Beauséjour.

There was even one—a very fat one—blocking the doorway of the hotel, and she smiled, thinking he wanted her, then recognized him and apologized.

He went up the badly lighted stairs, found the proprietress in the office, dressed this time in black silk with gold-rimmed spectacles, her hair a flaming red.

"Sit down. Excuse me a moment, will you?

"A towel for Number 17, Emma!"

She came back.

"Have you found anything new?"

"I'd like you to examine these photos carefully."

First he handed her the pictures of the handful of women Moers had picked out. She looked at them one by one, shook her head every time and passed the batch back to him.

"No. That's not the type at all. She's more refined than these women. Perhaps not exactly refined. What I mean is 'respectable.' Do you know what I'm getting at? She looks like a decent little woman, whereas the ones you've shown me might be women who come to this hotel."

"What about these?"

These were the dark-haired men. She was still shaking her head.

"No. That's not it at all. I don't know how to explain to you. These look too much like dagos. Monsieur Levine, you know, could have stayed at a big hotel in the Champs-Élysées without being conspicuous."

"And these?"

He handed her the last batch, sighing, and the minute she came to the third photograph she stiffened, casting a furtive little glance at the chief inspector. Was she reluctant to speak out?

"Is that him?"

"It may be. Wait till I take it to the light."

A girl was coming upstairs, with a client who kept to the darkest part of the staircase.

"Take Number 7, Clémence. The room's just been done."

She shifted her spectacles on her nose.

"I'd swear it's him. Yes. It's a pity he can't move. If I saw his walk, even from behind, I'd know him at once. But it's very unlikely that I'm mistaken."

On the back of the photograph Moers had written a résumé of the man's character, Maigret noted with interest that he was probably a Belgian, like the bookbinder. *Probably,* for he was known under several different names, and his true identity had never been established.

"Thank you."

"I hope you'll give me credit for this. I could very well have pretended not to recognize him. After all, they may be dangerous, and I'm taking a big risk."

She reeked so strongly of scent and the odors in the house were so cling'ng that he was glad to be back on the sidewalk breathing the smell of the rain-washed streets.

It was not yet seven o'clock. Little Lapointe must have gone to meet his sister and tell her what had happened at the Quai in the course of the day, just as Maigret had advised him to.

He was a good boy, still too easily upset, too emotional, but they could probably make something of him. Lucas, in his office, was still acting as orchestra conductor, keeping in touch by telephone with all departments, all sections of Paris and anywhere else where the trio might be found.

As for Janvier, he was still sticking to Alfonsi, who had gone back to the Rue de Turenne and stayed nearly an hour in the basement with Fernande.

The chief inspector drank another glass of beer while he read the notes written by Moers, which reminded him of something:

Alfred Moss. Belgian nationality (?). About 42.
Vaudeville artiste for about ten years.
Member of an acrobatic act on horizontal bars:
"Moss, Jeff and Joe."

Maigret was remembering. He was remembering particularly the one man of the three who played the clown in baggy black clothes and enormous shoes, with a blue chin, a huge red mouth and a green wig.

The man had seemed to be completely disjointed, and after each leap he would pretend to fall so heavily that it seemed impossible he hadn't broken something.

Has worked in most countries of Europe and even in the United States, where he was with Ringling Brothers' Circus for four years. Retired after an accident.

Then followed the names by which he had been known to the police since then: Mosselaer, Van Vlanderen, Paterson, Smith, Thomas . . . He had been arrested successively in Manchester, Brussels, Amsterdam, and three or four times in Paris.

However, he had never been convicted, for lack of proof. Whichever identity he was using, his papers were invariably in order, and he spoke four or five languages perfectly enough to change his nationality whenever it suited him.

The first time he had been prosecuted was in London, where he was claiming to be a Swiss citizen and working as an interpreter in a swank hotel. A jewel case had disappeared from a suite which he had been seen leaving, but the owner of the jewels, an old American lady, testified that she herself had summoned him to the suite to translate a letter she had received from Germany.

In Amsterdam four years later he had been suspected of being a con man. No proof could be established, any more than it could the first time, and he disappeared from circulation for a while.

General Surveillance in Paris was the next to take an interest in him, again unsuccessfully, during a period when the cross-frontier traffic in gold was being carried on on a big scale, and when Moss, now Joseph Thomas, was shuttling between France and Belgium.

He had his ups and downs, living now in a first-class, sometimes even a de luxe, hotel, sometimes in a shabby furnished room.

For three years there had been no record of him anywhere. It was not known in what country or under what name he was operating, assuming that he still was operating.

Maigret walked toward the telephone booth and got Lucas on the phone.

"Go up and see Moers and ask him for all the dope on a man named Moss. Yes. Tell him he's one of our boys. He'll give you his description and all the rest of it. Put out a general alarm. But he's not to be arrested. If he's found, they must try not to arouse his suspicion. Get it?"

"I get it, Chief. Someone's just spotted the child again."

"Where?"

"Avenue Denfert-Rochereau. I've sent someone over. I'm waiting. I haven't got enough men available any more. There's also been a call from the Gare du Nord. Torrence has gone over."

He felt like walking a bit in the rain and went through the Place d'Anvers, where he looked at the bench, now dripping with rain, where Madame Maigret had waited. Opposite, on the building at the corner of the Avenue Trudaine, there was a sign on which was written in big, faded letters the word "Dentist."

He would come back. There were so many things he wanted to do which the pressure always forced him to postpone to the next day.

He jumped on a bus. When he arrived at his own door he was astonished not to hear any sound from the kitchen, not to smell anything. He entered, went through the dining room, where the table wasn't set, and finally saw Madame Maigret in her slip engaged in taking off her stockings.

This was so unlike her that he didn't know what to say, and she burst out laughing when she saw his big round eyes.

"Are you cross, Maigret?"

Her voice held a tone of almost aggressive good humor which was quite new to him, and on the bed he could see her best dress and her Sunday hat.

"You'll have to be content with a cold dinner. Just imagine, I've been so busy that I haven't had time to prepare anything. Besides, you so seldom come home to meals nowadays!"

And sitting in her easy chair, she was rubbing her feet with a sigh of relief.

"I think I never walked so far in my life!"

He stood there, in his overcoat, with his wet hat on his head, looking at her and waiting. She was deliberately keeping him on tenterhooks.

"I began with the big stores although I was almost sure that was no use. But you never know, and I didn't want to regret my carelessness later. Then I did the whole of the Rue Lafayette. I went up the Rue Notre-Dame-de-Lorette and walked along the Rue Blanche and the Rue de Clichy. I came back down toward the Opéra—all this on foot, even after it had begun to rain. I suppose I may as well admit that yesterday, without telling you, I'd already done the Ternes area and the Champs-Élysées . . . just to make absolutely sure, because I suspected that it was too expensive around there."

At last he brought out the sentence she was waiting for, which she had been trying to elicit for quite a while.

"What were you looking for?"

"The hat, of course! Didn't you catch on? It was on my mind, that business. I thought it wasn't a man's job. A suit is a suit, especially a blue one. But a hat—that's different, and I'd had a good look at this one. They've been wearing white hats for several weeks now. Only one hat is never exactly like another. Do you see? You don't mind if dinner's cold, do you? I brought some cold stuff from the Italian place—Parma ham, pickled mushrooms and a whole lot of ready-to-eat hors d'oeuvres."

"What about the hat?"

"Are you interested in it, Maigret? By the way, your own is dripping on the carpet. You'd better take it off."

She had been successful, otherwise she wouldn't be in such a teasing mood and would never take the liberty of playing with him like ths. He would just have to let her take her time and maintain his grouchy expression, because she was enjoying it.

While she was putting on a woolen dress he sat down on the edge of the bed.

"I knew it wasn't a hat from a really first-class milliner and that there was no sense in looking in the Rue de la Paix, the Rue Saint-Honoré or the Avenue Matignon. Anyhow, those places don't put anything in the window, and I'd have had to go in and pretend to be a customer. Can you see me trying on hats at Caroline Reboux or Rose Valois?

"But it wasn't a hat from the Galeries or the Printemps either.

"Somewhere between the two. A hat from a milliner's definitely, and a milliner with good taste.

"That's why I did all the little shops, especially around the Place d'Anvers, or not too far away at all events.

"I saw at least a hundred white hats, and yet it was a pearl-gray one that finally stopped me, in the Rue Caumartin, at Hélène et Rosine's.

"It was exactly the same hat in another shade, and I'm sure I'm not mistaken. I told you that the one belonging to the lady with the little boy had a tiny veil, three or four fingers wide, that came down just over the eyes.

"The gray hat had the same veil."

"Did you go in?"

Maigret had to make an effort not to smile, for it was the first time that the shy Madame Maigret had taken part in an investigation, and no doubt also the first time she had entered a milliner's in the neighborhood of the Opéra.

"Are you surprised? Do you think I look too much of a homebody? Yes, I did go in. I was afraid it might be closed. I asked perfectly naturally if they didn't have the same hat in white.

"The lady said not, but they had it in pale blue, yellow

and jade green. She added that they had had it in white, but that they had sold it more than a month ago."

"What did you do?" he asked, intrigued.

"I heaved a deep sigh and said to her: 'That must have been the one I saw a friend of mine wearing.'

"I could see myself in the glass—because there are mirrors all around the shop—and my face was scarlet.

" 'Do you know Countess Panetti?' she asked with an astonishment that wasn't very complimentary.

" 'I've met her. I'd very much like to see her again, because I have some information for her which she asked me to get and I've mislaid her address.'

" 'I suppose she's still at . . .'

"She was on the point of stopping. She wasn't completely sure of me. But she couldn't very well not finish her sentence.

" 'I suppose she's still at Claridge's.' "

Madame Maigret was looking at him triumphantly and teasingly at the same time, but with an anxious trembling of her lips in spite of everything. He kept up the game to the end and muttered:

"I hope you didn't go interrogating the bell captain at Claridge's."

"I came straight back. Are you cross?"

"No."

"I've caused you enough trouble with this business. The least I can do is try to help you. Now come and eat. I hope you're going to take time for a bite before you go over there."

This dinner reminded him of their first meals together, when she was discovering Paris and was delighted by all the little ready-to-eat items sold in the Italian shops. It was more like a picnic than a dinner.

"Do you think the information's reliable?"

"So long as you didn't get the wrong hat."

"I'm absolutely sure about that. As far as the shoes go, I'm not so confident."

"What's this about shoes now?"

"When you're sitting on a park bench, your eyes naturally fall on the shoes of the person next to you. Once when I looked at them closely I could see that she was embarrassed and was trying to stick her feet under the bench."

"Why?"

"I'll explain, Maigret. Don't make that face! It's not your fault if you don't know anything about feminine matters. Suppose someone accustomed to first-class couturiers wants to look like a little housewife and be inconspicuous. She buys a ready-made suit, which is easy. She may also buy a hat that isn't in the luxury class, although I'm not quite so sure about the hat."

"What do you mean?"

"She may already have had it and thought it looked enough like the other white hats being worn this season by shopgirls. She takes off her jewelry, certainly! But there's one thing she would have a lot of trouble getting used to: ready-made shoes. Having your shoes custommade by the best bootmakers makes your feet delicate. You've heard me groaning often enough to know that women have sensitive feet by nature. So the lady keeps her own shoes, thinking no one will notice them. That's where she's wrong, because as far as I'm concerned that's the first thing I look at. Usually it happens the other way round: you see pretty, well-dressed women with expensive frocks or fur coats wearing cheap shoes."

"Did she have expensive shoes?"

"Custom-made, I'm sure. I don't know enough about it to say where they came from. No doubt some women could have told."

He took time after dinner to pour himself a little glass of *prunelle* and to smoke almost a whole pipe.

"Are you going to Claridge's? You won't be too late?"

He took a cab, got out opposite the luxury hotel on the Champs-Élysées and walked over to the bell captain's office. It was the night man by this time, whom he had known for years, and this was a good thing because night bell captains invariably know more about the guests than those on the day shift.

His arrival in a place of this type always produced the same effect. He could see the clerks at the reception desk, the assistant manager and even the elevator boys raising their eyebrows and wondering what was up. Scandals are unpopular in a luxury hotel, and the presence of a chief inspector from the Police Judiciaire rarely bodes any good.

"How are you, Benoît?"

"Not too bad, Monsieur Maigret. The Americans are beginning to show up."

"Is Countess Panetti still here?"

"It's at least a month since she left. Would you like me to check the exact date?"

"Did her family go with her?"

"What family?"

It was the slack time. Most of the guests were out, at the theater or at dinner. In the golden light the bellboys stood, with their arms dangling, near the marble columns and observed the chief inspector, whom they all knew by sight, from a distance.

"I never knew she had any family. She's been stopping here for years now, and——"

"Tell me, have you ever seen the countess in a white hat?"

"Certainly. She received one a few days before her departure."

"Did she also wear a blue suit?"

"No. You must have got them mixed up, Monsieur Maigret. The blue suit is her maid, or her companion if you prefer it—in any case the young lady who travels with her."

"You've never seen Countess Panetti in a blue suit?"

"If you knew her you wouldn't ask me that."

Just on the chance, Maigret handed him the photographs of the women picked out by Moers.

"Anyone there who looks like her?"

Benoît looked at the chief inspector, flabbergasted.

"Are you sure you're not mistaken? You're showing me photographs of women under thirty, and the countess isn't much less than seventy. Listen, you'd better find out what your colleagues in the Night Life Squad have got on her, because they must know her.

"We get all kinds, don't we? Oh, well! The countess is one of our most unusual guests."

"In the first place, do you know who she is?"

"She's the widow of Count Panetti, the munitions and heavy industry man in Italy. She lives all over the place—Paris, Cannes, Egypt. I think she spends some time every year in Vichy, too."

"Does she drink?"

"Shall we say she uses champagne instead of water? I wouldn't be surprised if she brushed her teeth with Pommery *brut!* She dresses like a young girl, makes up like a doll and spends most of every night in night clubs."

"Her maid?"

"I don't know much about her. She's always getting new ones. I haven't seen this one until this year. Last year she had a big girl with red hair, a professional masseuse, because she used to take a massage every day."

"Do you know the girl's name?"

"Gloria something. I haven't got her slip any more, but they'll know in the office. I don't know if she's Italian or just from the South, possibly even from Toulouse."

"Small and dark?"

"Yes. Well dressed, well mannered, pretty. I didn't see much of her. She lived in the suite, not in a servant's room, and she had her meals with her employer."

"No man?"

"Only the son-in-law who came to see them from time to time."

"When?"

"Not long before they left. Ask the desk for the date. He didn't live in the hotel."

"Do you know his name?"

"Krynker, I think. He's Czech or Hungarian."

"Dark, rather heavy, around forty?"

"No. On the contrary, very fair and much younger. I doubt that he's more than thirty."

They were interrupted by a group of American women in evening dress depositing their keys and asking for a taxi.

"As for swearing that he was really a son-in-law . . ."

"Did she have affairs?"

"I don't know. I can't answer yes or no."

"Did the son-in-law ever spend the night here?"

"No. But they went out together several times."

"With the companion?"

"She never went out at night with the countess. I've never even seen her in evening dress."

"Do you know where they went?"

"To London, if I remember right. But just a minute. Something's coming back to me. Ernest! Come here. There's nothing to be afraid of. Didn't Countess Panetti leave her heavy luggage behind?"

"Yes, sir."

The bell captain explained:

"It often happens that our clients who are going away for a fairly long time leave some of their luggage here. We have a special baggage room for it. The countess left her trunks there."

"She didn't say when she would be back?"

"Not that I know of."

"Did she leave alone?"

"With her maid."

"In a taxi?"

"You'd have to ask my opposite number on the day shift about that. You'll find him here tomorrow morning from eight o'clock on."

Maigret took out of his pocket the photograph of Moss. The bell captain merely glanced at it and pulled a face.

"You won't find him here."

"Do you know him?"

"Paterson. I did know him, under the name of Mosselaer, when I was working in Milan at least fifteen years ago. He's barred from all the luxury hotels and he wouldn't dare show his face in them. He knows they wouldn't give him a room, wouldn't even allow him to walk across the lobby."

"You haven't seen him recently?"

"No. If I did run into him I'd start by asking him for the hundred lira he borrowed from me years ago and never returned."

"Does the day man have a telephone?"

"You can always try to call him at his villa at Saint-Cloud, but he hardly ever answers. He doesn't like to be disturbed in the evening and he usually takes the phone off the hook."

Nevertheless he did answer, and the music from the radio was audible in the telephone too.

"The head baggage porter could give you more accurate information, I'm sure. I don't remember having a cab called for her. Generally, when she leaves the hotel, she gets me to look after her train or plane tickets."

"You didn't do so this time?"

"No. It's only just struck me. Maybe she left in a private car."

"You don't know whether the son-in-law, Krynker, owned a car?"

"He certainly did! A big chocolate-colored American one."

"Thank you. I'll probably see you tomorrow morning."

He went over to the desk, where the assistant manager

in his black coat and striped trousers insisted on finding the slips himself.

"She left the hotel on February 16, during the evening. I have her bill right here."

"Was she alone?"

"I see two luncheons down for that day. So she must have eaten with her companion."

"Would you please lend me this bill?"

It showed the daily expenditures of the countess at the hotel, and Maigret wanted to study them at leisure.

"On condition you give it back to me! Otherwise we'll be in trouble with the income tax boys. By the way, how do the police come to be interested in a personality like Countess Panetti?"

Maigret, his mind on something else, almost replied: "All because of my wife!"

He caught himself in time and muttered:

"I don't know yet. Something about a hat."

# 6

# THE LAUNDRY BOAT ON THE SEINE

MAIGRET WAS PUSHING the revolving door, catching sight of the garlands of lights on the Champs-Élysées which, in the rain, had always reminded him of moist eyes; he was about to start walking down to the Rond Point when he raised his eyebrows. Leaning against a tree trunk, not far from a flower girl who was sheltering from the rain, Janvier was watching him, pathetic, comical, looking as if he were trying to get something across to him.

Maigret walked up to him.

"What in the world are you doing here?"

The inspector indicated a silhouette outlined against one of the few illuminated shopwindows. It was Alfonsi, who seemed intensely interested in a display of luggage.

"He's following you. So that I happen to be following you too."

"Did he see Liotard after his visit to the Rue de Turenne?"

"No. He phoned him."

"Call it a day. Do you want me to drop you at home?"

Janvier lived not far out of his way, in the Rue Réaumur.

Alfonsi watched them walk off together, seemed surprised, taken aback, then, as Maigret was hailing a cab, decided to turn back and went off in the direction of the Étoile.

"Anything new?" Janvier asked.

"Any amount. Too much, almost."

"Do you want me to take care of Alfonsi again tomorrow morning?"

"No. Drop by the office. There'll probably be plenty of work for everybody."

When the inspector had got out Maigret said to the driver:

"Drive through the Rue de Turenne."

It wasn't late. He vaguely hoped he would see a light at the bookbinder's.

This would have been the ideal time for the long chat with Fernande that he had been hankering after for quite a while.

Because of a reflection on the glass door he got out of the cab but realized that the interior was in darkness, hesitated to knock and set off again in the direction of the Quai des Orfèvres, where Torrence was on duty, and gave him some instructions.

Madame Maigret had just gone to bed when he tiptoed in. As he was undressing in the dark so as not to wake her she asked:

"The hat?"

"It was bought by Countess Panetti all right."

"Did you see her?"

"No, but she's about seventy-five."

He went to bed in a bad temper, or preoccupied, and it was still raining when he awoke. Then he cut himself while shaving.

"Are you going on with your investigation?" he asked his wife, who, in curlers, was serving his breakfast.

"Is there anything else for me to do?" she inquired seriously.

"I don't know. Now that you've started . . ."

He bought his paper at the corner of the Boulevard Voltaire, found in it no new manifesto by Philippe Liotard, no new challenge. The night bell captain at Claridge's had been discreet, for there was no mention of the countess either.

Back at the Quai, Lucas, relieving Torrence, had received his instructions, and the machine was functioning. They were now looking for the Italian countess on the Riviera and in foreign capitals, while inquiries were also being made about the man named Krynker and the maid.

On the bus platform, enveloped in fine rain, a passenger facing him was reading his paper, and this paper carried a headline which gave the chief inspector something to think about:

## INQUIRY DRAGS

How many people, at that very minute, were actively engaged on it? Railway stations, ports, airports were still under observation. Hotels and rooming houses were continuously being searched. Not only in Paris and in France, but in London, Brussels, Amsterdam, Rome, they were trying to pick up the track of Alfred Moss.

Maigret got out at the Rue de Turenne, entered the Tabac des Vosges to buy a packet of tobacco and took the opportunity of drinking a glass of white wine. There were no reporters, nothing but local residents who were beginning to pull in their horns a bit.

The bookbinder's door was locked. He knocked and soon saw Fernande emerging from the basement by the spiral staircase. In curlers, like Madame Maigret, she hesitated when she recognized him through the glass, and finally came and opened the door.

"I'd like to talk to you for a few minutes."

It was chilly on the stairs, since the furnace had not been relighted.

"Wouldn't you rather come downstairs?"

He followed her into the kitchen, which she had been in the middle of cleaning when he disturbed her.

She, too, seemed tired, with something like discouragement in her expression.

"Would you like a cup of coffee? I have some hot."

He accepted, sat down by the table, and she finally sat down facing him, wrapping the skirts of her bathrobe around her bare legs.

"Alfonsi came to see you yesterday. What does he want?"

"I don't know. He's interested mainly in the questions you ask me and he keeps telling me not to trust you."

"Did you mention the poisoning attempt to him?"

"Yes."

"Why?"

"You didn't tell me not to. I can't remember how it came up. He's working for Liotard, and it seems all right for him to be kept informed."

"No one else has been to see you?"

It seemed to him that she hesitated, but it may have been the effect of the weariness weighing upon the wife of the man from Flanders. She had helped herself to a big cup of coffee. She probably relied on black coffee in copious amounts to keep her going.

"No. Nobody."

"Did you tell your husband why you're not bringing his meals any more?"

"I managed to let him know. I appreciate what you did."

"No one's called you?"

"No. I don't think so. I hear the bell occasionally, but by the time I get upstairs there's no one on the line."

Then he took from his pocket the photograph of Alfred Moss.

"Do you recognize this man?"

She looked at the photograph, then at Maigret, and said quite naturally:

"Of course."

"Who is it?"

"It's Alfred, my husband's brother."

"Is it long since you've seen him?"

"I hardly ever see him. Sometimes he doesn't come here in more than a year. He lives abroad most of the time."

"Do you know what he does?"

"Not exactly. Frans says he's an unfortunate character, a failure, who never had a break."

"He never mentioned his profession?"

"I know he worked in a circus. He was an acrobat and he broke his spine in a fall."

"And since then?"

"Isn't he some kind of impresario?"

"Did you know he didn't call himself Steuvels like his brother but Moss? Have you ever been told why?"

"Yes."

She was reluctant to go on, looked at the picture which Maigret had left on the kitchen table near the coffee cups, then she got up to turn off the gas under a pan of water.

"I couldn't help guessing part of it. Perhaps if you questioned Frans on this subject he'd tell you more. You know that his parents were very poor, but that's not the whole story. Actually his mother was in the business I used to be in myself—at Gand, or rather in a shady district just outside the town.

"She drank, into the bargain. I wonder if she wasn't half crazy. She had seven or eight children and half the time she didn't know who their father was.

"It was Frans who chose the name Steuvels later. His mother was called Mosselaer."

"Is she dead?"

"I think so. He avoids mentioning her."

"Has he kept in touch with his brothers and sisters?"

"I don't think so. Alfred's the only one who comes to see him from time to time—rarely. He must have his ups and downs because sometimes he seems prosperous: he's well dressed, gets out of a cab in front of the house and brings presents, while other times he's quite shabby."

"When did you last see him?"

"Let me think. It must be two months ago at least."

"Did he stay to dinner?"

"Yes. He always did."

"Tell me, on the occasion of these visits, did your husband ever try to get rid of you under any pretext?"

"No. Why? They were sometimes in the workshop by themselves, but from downstairs, where I was cooking, I could hear what they said."

"What did they talk about?"

"Nothing particular. Alfred liked to reminisce about the time when he was an acrobat and the different countries he'd lived in. And he was also the one who nearly always made allusions to their childhood and their mother. That's where I got the little information I have."

"Alfred is the younger, I suppose?"

"Three or four years younger. Afterward Frans would sometimes walk to the corner of the street with him. That's the only time I wasn't with them."

"They never talked business?"

"Never."

"Alfred never came with friends either, male or female?"

"He was always alone. I think he'd married once. I'm not sure. It seems to me he mentioned it. In any case, he'd been in love with a woman and she'd made him unhappy."

It was warm and quiet in the little kitchen, from which you couldn't see the outside world at all and where the light had to be kept on all day. Maigret would have liked to have Frans Steuvels there facing him and to talk to him as he was talking to his wife.

"You told me last time I was here that he practically never went out without you. Yet he went to the bank from time to time."

"I don't call that going out. It's just around the corner. He only had to walk across the Place des Vosges."

"Otherwise you were together from morning to night?"

"Just about. I'd go marketing, of course, but always close by. Once in a blue moon I'd go downtown to do some shopping. I'm not very stylish, as you may have noticed."

"You never went to see relatives?"

"I only have my mother and my sister at Concarneau, and it took a fake telegram to get me to go and visit them."

It was as though something were bothering Maigret.

"There's no day when you're regularly out?"

"No. Except for wash day, of course."

"You don't do the washing here?"

"Where could I do it? I have to go up to the ground floor for water. I can't hang up the washing in the work-shop, and it wouldn't dry in a basement. Once a week in summer and once a fortnight in winter I go to the laundry boat on the Seine."

"Whereabouts?"

"Place du Vert-Galant. You know, just below the Pont Neuf. It takes me half a day. The next morning I go to fetch the washing, which is dry and ready to iron."

Visibly Maigret was relaxing, smoking his pipe with more pleasure, and his expression had become livelier.

"In fact, one day a week in summer, one day every two weeks in winter, Frans was alone here?"

"Not all day."

"Did you go to the laundry boat in the morning or the afternoon?"

"Afternoon. I tried going in the morning, but it was difficult on account of the cleaning and cooking."

"Do you have a key to the house?"

"Of course."

"Did you often have to use it?"

"What do you mean?"

"Did it sometimes happen that when you came back your husband wasn't in the workshop?"

"Hardly ever."

"But it did happen?"

"I think so. Yes."

"Recently?"

She had just thought of it, too, for she hesitated.

"The week I went to Concarneau."

"When's your wash day?"

"Monday."

"Did he come home long after you?"

"Not long. Maybe an hour."

"Did you ask him where he'd been?"

"I never ask him anything. He's free. It's not my place to ask him questions."

"You don't know whether he left the neighborhood? Weren't you worried?"

"I was at the door when he came back. I saw him get out of the bus on the corner of the Rue des Francs-Bourgeois."

"The bus coming from downtown or from the Bastille?"

"From downtown."

"So far as I can tell from this photo, the two brothers are the same height?"

"Yes. Alfred looks slimmer because he has a thin face, but his body is more muscular. They're not alike in features, except that they both have red hair. But from behind the resemblance is striking, and I've occasionally mistaken one for the other."

"The times when you saw Alfred, how was he dressed?"

"That depended. I've told you already."

"Do you think he may have borrowed money from his brother?"

"I've thought of that, but it doesn't seem very likely. Not in front of me, in any case."

"On his last visit wasn't he wearing a blue suit?"

She looked him in the eye. She had caught on.

"I'm almost sure he was wearing something dark, but gray rather than blue. When you live by artificial light you don't pay much attention to colors."

"How did you manage about money, you and your husband?"

"What money?"

"Did he give you housekeeping money every month?"

"No. When I ran out I'd ask him for some."

"He never protested?"

She turned slightly pink.

"He was absent-minded. He always thought he'd given me money just the day before. And then he'd say in astonishment: 'What, again?' "

"What about your personal things—dresses and hats?"

"I don't spend much. You know that."

It was her turn to put some questions to him, as if she had been waiting a long time for this moment.

"Listen, Chief Inspector. I'm not very intelligent, but I'm not so stupid either. You've questioned me; your detectives have questioned me, and the journalists too, not to mention the tradesmen and the neighbors. A young gentleman of seventeen who plays amateur detective even stopped me in the street and asked me some questions he had written down in a little notebook. Once and for all, tell me honestly: do you think Frans is guilty?"

"Guilty of what?"

"You know perfectly well: of having killed a man and burned the body in the furnace."

He hesitated. He could have given her any answer that came into his head, but he was determined to be honest.

"I have no idea."

"In that case why is he being kept in prison?"

"In the first place, that's not my responsibility but the examining magistrate's. And then you mustn't forget that all the circumstantial evidence is against him."

"The teeth!" she flashed, with irony.

"And above all the bloodstains on the blue suit. Don't forget the suitcase that vanished either."

"And that I never saw!"

"That doesn't make any difference. Other people saw it—at least a detective did. And then there's the fact that you were called out of town, as if by chance, at that very moment, by a fake telegram. Now, between you and me, I admit that if it were up to me I'd prefer to let your husband go, but I'd hesitate to release him for the sake of his own safety. You saw what happened yesterday."

"Yes. That's just what I'm thinking about."

"Whether he's guilty or innocent, he seems to be in somebody's way."

"Why did you bring me the photo of his brother?"

"Because, in spite of what you think, that man is quite a dangerous criminal."

"Has he committed murder?"

"Probably not. That type of man hardly ever kills. But he's wanted by the police of three or four countries, and for more than fifteen years he's been living by stealing and swindling. Are you surprised?"

"No."

"Did you suspect it?"

"When Frans told me his brother was unfortunate, it seemed to me that he wasn't using the word 'unfortunate' in its usual sense. Do you think that Alfred would have been capable of kidnaping a child?"

"I tell you again I have no idea. By the way, have you ever heard of Countess Panetti?"

"Who's she?"

"A very rich Italian woman who lived at Claridge's."

"Has she been killed too?"

"It's possible, and it's also possible that she's simply away spending the carnival season at Cannes or Nice. I'll know tonight. I'd like to take another look at your husband's accounts."

"Come this way. I've got loads of questions to ask you, but they've slipped my mind. It's when you're not here that I think of them. I ought to write them down like the young man playing detective."

She let him precede her downstairs and brought from a shelf a big black book which the police had examined five or six times.

At the very end an index contained the names of the bookbinder's clients, old and new, in alphabetical order. The name Panetti was not listed. Neither was Krynker.

Steuvels had fine, jerky handwriting, with some letters overlapping others and a peculiar way of making the *r*'s and *t*'s.

"You've never heard the name Krynker?"

"Not that I remember. Look, we would be together the whole day, but I never assumed the right to ask him questions. Sometimes you seem to forget, Chief Inspector, that I'm not just an ordinary wife. Remember where he found me. His action has always amazed me. And now it suddenly occurs to me, as a result of our conversation, that the reason he did it may have been that he remembered what his mother had been."

Maigret, as if he were no longer listening, strode toward the door, flung it open and seized Alfonsi by the collar of his camel-hair coat.

"Come here, you. You're at it again. Have you decided to spend your days dogging my heels?"

The other man tried to brazen it out, but the chief inspector had a strong grip on the scruff of his neck and was shaking him like a puppet.

"What are you doing here? You'd better tell me."

"I was waiting for you to leave."

"To come pestering this woman?"

"I have a right to. Provided she chooses to receive me. . . ."

"What are you after?"

"Ask Maître Liotard."

"The hell with Liotard! Let me tell you one thing. If I catch you following me again I'll have you pinched for living off a prostitute. Understand?"

This wasn't an empty threat. Maigret knew very well that the woman Alfonsi lived with spent most of her evenings in Montmartre night clubs and that she was not unwilling to accompany visiting foreigners to their hotels.

When he came back to Fernande he looked relieved, and the figure of the ex-detective could be seen making off in the rain toward the Place des Vosges.

"What sort of questions does he ask you?"

"Always the same. He wants to know what you ask me, what I've told you, what you're interested in, what objects you've examined."

"I think he'll let you alone in future."

"Do you think Maître Liotard is harming my husband?"

"Whether he is or not, we can't do anything about it at this point."

He had to go back downstairs, because he had left the photograph of Moss on the kitchen table. Instead of making for the Quai des Orfèvres, he crossed the street and entered the shoemaker's shop.

The latter, at nine in the morning, already had several drinks under his belt and reeked of white wine.

"Well, Chief Inspector, everything going all right?"

The two shops were exactly opposite one another. The shoemaker and the bookbinder could not help seeing each other every time they raised their eyes, both hunched over their work, with only the width of the street between them.

"Can you remember some of the bookbinder's clients?"

"A few. Yes."

"This one?"

He held the photograph under his nose, while Fernande, opposite, watched them anxiously.

"I call him the clown."

"Why?"

"I don't know. Because I think he looks like a clown."

Suddenly he scratched his head, seemed to make a welcome discovery.

"Look here, stand me a drink, and I'll make it worth your while. It was a bit of good luck that you showed me that picture. I mentioned a clown and all of a sudden the word made me think of a suitcase. Why? Well, obviously because clowns usually come into the ring with a suitcase."

"You mean the stooges, don't you?"

"Stooges or clowns, it's the same thing. How about a drink?"

"Later."

"You don't trust me? You're wrong. Honest as a newborn babe, that's what I always say. Well, anyhow, there's no doubt that the fellow with the suitcase is your man."

"What fellow with the suitcase?"

The shoemaker gave him a wink which tried to be knowing.

"You're not going to get cute with me, are you? I suppose I don't read the papers, do I? Well, what were the papers concerned with at the beginning? Didn't people come asking me whether I'd seen Frans go out with a suitcase, or his wife, or anyone else?"

"And you did see the man in the photo go out with a suitcase?"

"Not that day. Anyhow, not that I noticed. But I'm thinking of the other times."

"Did he come here often?"

"Yes, often."

"Once a week, for example? Or once a fortnight?"

"Maybe. I don't want to make anything up because I know what a rough time the lawyers'll give me if this ever comes up in court. He used to come here often, and that's all I'm saying."

"In the morning? Afternoon?"

"My answer to that is: the afternoon. Do you know why? Because I can remember seeing him when the lights were on, so it must have been afternoon. He always had a small suitcase with him."

"Brown?"

"Probably. Aren't most suitcases brown? He would sit down in a corner of the shop, waiting for the work to be finished, and he'd leave again with the suitcase."

"Did that take long?"

"I don't know. More than an hour in any case. Sometimes it seemed to me that he stayed the whole afternoon."

"Did he always come on the same day?"

"I can't tell you that either."

"Think before you answer. Did you ever see this man in the studio at the same time as Madame Steuvels?"

"At the same time as Fernande? Wait. I can't call it to mind. Once, at least, the two men went out together, and Frans closed his shop."

"Recently?"

"I'll have to think. When are we going to have that drink?"

Maigret had no alternative but to follow him to the Grand Turenne, where the shoemaker assumed a triumphant manner.

"Two old brandies. On the chief inspector."

He drank three, one after another, and was trying to start the business of the clown all over again by the time Maigret managed to get rid of him. When he passed the bookbinder's studio Fernande was watching him through the glass door with an air of reproach.

But he had to keep on with his job to the end. He entered the apartment of the concierge, who was busy peeling potatoes.

"Well, well. So you're back!" she observed tartly, offended at having been neglected for so long.

"Do you know this man?"

She went to fetch her glasses from the drawer.

"I don't know his name, if that's what you want, but I've seen him before. Didn't the shoemaker give you the information?"

She was jealous because other people had been questioned first.

"Have you seen him often?"

"I've seen him, that's all I know."

"Was he a client of the bookbinder?"

"I suppose so, seeing he came to his shop."

"He didn't come on any other occasions?"

"I think he occasionally came to dinner with them, but I pay so little attention to my tenants!"

The stationer across the street, the cardboard manufacturer, the umbrella woman, in short, the routine—always the same question, the same gesture, the picture, which people examined gravely. Some hesitated. Others had seen the man without remembering where or in what circumstances.

Just as he was leaving the neighborhood Maigret had an impulse to push open the door of the Tabac des Vosges one last time.

"Have you ever seen that mug before, boss?"

The bartender did not hesitate.

"The man with the suitcase," he said.

"Explain."

"I don't know what he sells, but he must be a door-to-door salesman. He used to come in quite often, always a little while after lunch. He'd drink strawberry syrup with Vichy water and he explained to me that he had a stomach ulcer."

"Would he stay long?"

"Sometimes a quarter of an hour, sometimes longer. Look, he always sat there, near the door."

From where he could keep an eye on the corner of the Rue de Turenne!

"He must have been waiting till it was time for an appointment with a customer. Once, not so long ago, he stayed almost an hour and finally asked for a telephone token."

"You don't know who he called?"

"No. When he came back it was only to leave again right away."

"In which direction?"

"I wasn't paying attention."

As a reporter was coming in, the proprietor asked Maigret in an undertone:

"Is it all right to talk about it?"

Maigret shrugged. There was no point in making mysteries, now that the shoemaker was in the know.

"If you want to."

When he entered Lucas' office the latter was coping with two telephones, and Maigret had to wait quite a while.

"I'm still hunting for the countess," sighed the sergeant, mopping his forehead. "The Wagons-Lits Company, who know her quite well, haven't seen her on any of their lines for several months. I've had most of the big hotels at Cannes, Nice, Antibes and Villefranche on the line. Nothing doing. I've also talked to the casinos, where she hasn't set foot. Lapointe, who speaks English, is telephoning Scotland Yard right now, and someone or other is taking care of the Italians."

Before going in to see Judge Dossin, Maigret went upstairs to have a word with Moers and return the useless photographs.

"No results?" asked poor Moers.

"One out of three, and that's not bad. Now we only

have to round up the other two, but it's possible that they've never been through the Identification Department."

At noon they were still not on the track of Countess Panetti, and two Italian journalists who had been tipped off were waiting, greatly excited, outside the door to Maigret's office.

# 7

## MAIGRET'S SUNDAY

MADAME MAIGRET had been rather surprised when on Saturday, about three o'clock, her husband telephoned to find out whether dinner was cooking.

"Not yet. Why? Yes, of course I'd like to. If you're sure you'll be free. Quite sure? All right. I'll get dressed. I'll be there. Near the clock, yes. No, no sauerkraut for me, but I'd love a *potée lorraine*. What? You're not joking, are you? Are you serious, Maigret? Anywhere I like? That's too good to be true, and I feel sure you're going to call me back in an hour to tell me you won't be home to dinner or till morning. Oh, well! I'll get ready anyway."

So that instead of smelling of cooking that Saturday the apartment on the Boulevard Richard-Lenoir had smelled of bath water, cologne and the sweetish perfume which Madame Maigret kept for special occasions.

Maigret was at the meeting place almost on time—within five minutes—at the Alsatian restaurant in the Rue d'En-ghien where they sometimes had dinner, and, relaxed, with the air of thinking about the same things as other men, he ate sauerkraut prepared just the way he liked it.

"Have you decided on the movie?"

Because—and this was what had made Madame Maigret

so incredulous on the telephone—he had invited her to
spend the evening at any movie theater she chose.

They went to the Paramount on the Boulevard des
Italiens, and the chief inspector stood in line for the tickets
without grumbling, emptying his pipe in an enormous
spittoon in passing.

They heard electronic organs, saw the orchestra emerge
from the bowels of the earth on a platform while a curtain
transformed itself into a sort of synthetic sunset. It was not
until after the cartoons that Madame Maigret understood.
The preview of the coming movie had just been shown,
then some short reels advertising some kind of candy and
furniture on the installment plan.

### POLICE HEADQUARTERS INFORM US . . .

It was the first time she had seen such a notice on the
screen, and immediately afterward a rogues' gallery photograph was projected, first full face, then in profile—the
photograph of Alfred Moss, whose successive aliases were
listed.

### ANYBODY HAVING SEEN THIS MAN IN THE COURSE OF THE LAST TWO MONTHS IS REQUESTED TO TELEPHONE IMMEDIATELY. . . .

"So that was it?" she said, out in the street again, while
they were walking part of the way home in order to get
some fresh air.

"That wasn't the only reason. And by the way the idea
isn't mine. It was suggested to the director ages ago, but
there had never been an opportunity to try it out until now.
Moers had noticed that photographs published in the papers
are always more or less distorted because of the
half-tone screen and the inking. Film projection, on the

other hand, by enlarging the smallest characteristics, makes a more striking impression."

"Well, anyway, whether that was the reason or not, it turned out nicely for me. How long is it since we did this?"

"Three weeks," he said in all sincerity.

"Exactly two and a half months!"

They squabbled a bit, in fun. And next morning, because of the sun, which was again brilliant and springlike, Maigret sang in the bathtub. He walked all the way to the Quai, through almost deserted streets, and it was always a pleasure to find the wide corridors of Police Headquarters with their doors standing open on vacant offices.

Lucas had only just arrived. Torrence was there too; so was Janvier; it wasn't long before little Lapointe appeared, but because it was Sunday they seemed to be working like amateurs. Perhaps it was also because it was Sunday that they left the communicating doors open, and from time to time, by way of music, they heard the bells of the local churches.

Lapointe was the only one who had brought in any new information. The previous night, before leaving, Maigret had asked him:

"By the way, where does that young journalist live who's flirting with your sister?"

"He's not flirting with her any more. You mean Antoine Bizard."

"They've broken up?"

"I don't know. Maybe he's afraid of me."

"I'd like his address."

"I don't know it. I know where he eats most of his meals and I doubt that my sister knows any more. I'll inquire at the paper."

As he entered, he had handed a slip of paper to Maigret. This was the address in question, Rue Bergère, in the same apartment house as Philippe Liotard.

"That's fine, son. Thanks," the chief inspector said simply, without adding any comment.

If it had been a bit warmer he would have taken off his coat just for the sake of being in his shirt sleeves like people who putter around all day on Sunday, for puttering around was just what he felt like doing. All his pipes were lined up on his desk, and he took out of his pocket his fat black notebook, which he always stuffed full of notes but practically never consulted.

Two or three times he threw into the wastebasket the big sheets of paper, ruled into columns to start with, on which he had scribbled, then changed his mind.

In the end his work took a turn for the better.

*Thursday, February 15*—Countess Panetti, accompanied by her maid, Gloria Lotti, leaves Claridge's in the chocolate-colored Chrysler of her son-in-law Krynker.

The date had been confirmed by the bell captain on the day shift. As for the car, the information had been furnished by one of the hotel bellboys who had reported the time of departure as seven o'clock at night. He had added that the old lady seemed worried and that her son-in-law was hurrying her as if they were about to miss a train or an important appointment.

Still no trace of the countess. He went into Lucas' office to make sure. The sergeant was still receiving reports from all over the place.

The Italian journalists had obtained only a few scraps of information from the police the night before and had furnished a few themselves. They did in fact know Countess Panetti. The marriage of her only daughter Bella had caused a big stir in Italy because, lacking her mother's consent, the girl had run away from home to get married at Monte Carlo.

That was five years ago, and since then the two families never met.

If Krynker was in Paris, said the Italian journalists, it was probably to attempt another reconciliation.

*Friday, February 16*—Gloria Lotti, who is wearing the countess' white hat, goes to Concarneau from where she sends a telegram to Fernande Steuvels and from where she returns the same night without having met anyone.

In the margin Maigret had amused himself by drawing a woman's hat with a tiny veil.

*Saturday, February 17*—At noon Fernande leaves the Rue de Turenne and departs for Concarneau. Her husband does not accompany her to the station. About four o'clock a client comes to call for some work he has commissioned and finds Frans Steuvels in his workshop, where nothing seems out of the ordinary. Asked about the suitcase, he doesn't remember having seen it.

At a few minutes past eight three persons, among them Alfred Moss and probably the man who is later to register in the Rue Lepic under the name of Levine, are taken by taxi from the Gare Saint-Lazare to the corner of the Rue de Turenne and the Rue des Francs-Bourgeois.

The concierge hears knocking at Steuvels' door just before nine o'clock. She has the impression that the three men entered.

In the margin, in red pencil, he wrote: "Is the third character Krynker?"

*Sunday, February 18*—The furnace, not in use for the last few days, was going all night, and Frans Steuvels has to make at least five trips into the courtyard to carry out the ashes to the garbage cans.

Mademoiselle Béguin, the tenant on the fifth floor, was inconvenienced by the smoke, "which had a funny smell."

*Monday, February 19*—The furnace is still going. The bookbinder is at home alone all day.

*Tuesday, February 20*—The Police Judiciaire receives an anonymous note about a man having been burned in the bookbinder's furnace. Fernande returns from Concarneau.

*Wednesday, February 21*—Lapointe's visit to the Rue de Turenne. He sees the suitcase with the handle mended with string under a table in the workshop. Lapointe leaves the studio about noon. Has lunch with his sister and talks to her about the case. Does Mademoiselle Lapointe meet her young man, Antoine Bizard, who lives in the same building as the briefless lawyer Liotard? Or does she telephone him?

In the afternoon, before five, the lawyer calls at the Rue de Turenne under the pretext of ordering a bookplate.

When Lucas makes his search, at five o'clock, the suitcase has disappeared.

Interrogation of Steuvels at Police Headquarters. Toward the end of the night he names Maître Liotard as his lawyer.

Maigret stood up for a little stroll and a glance at the

notes the inspectors were taking at the telephones. It wasn't time yet to have beer sent up, and he simply filled another pipe instead.

*Thursday, February 22—*

*Friday, February 23—*

*Saturday . . .*

A whole column of dates with nothing opposite them, except that the inquiry was dragging; the papers were agitating; Liotard, snapping like a stray dog, was attacking the police in general and Maigret in particular. The right-hand column remained empty until:

*Sunday, March 10*—A man named Levine rents a room at the Hôtel Beauséjour in the Rue Lepic and moves in with a little boy of about two.

Gloria Lotti, who passes for the nursemaid, looks after the child, whom she takes out every morning for an airing in the Place d'Anvers while Levine is asleep.

She does not stay all night at the hotel, which she leaves very late when Levine comes home.

*Monday, March 11*—Ditto.

*Tuesday, March 12*—Half past nine. Gloria and the child leave the Hôtel Beauséjour as usual. Quarter past ten. Moss appears at the hotel and asks for Levine. The latter immediately packs and brings down his luggage while Moss remains alone in the room.

Five minutes to eleven. Gloria sees Levine and instantly leaves the child, who remains in the charge of Mme. Maigret.

A little after eleven she enters the Beauséjour with her companion. They join Moss and all three of them argue for more than an hour. Moss leaves first. About one Gloria and Levine leave the hotel and Gloria gets into a cab alone.

She goes back to the Place d'Anvers and picks up the child.

She takes the cab as far as the Porte de Neuilly, then says she wants to go to the Gare Saint-Lazare and suddenly stops in the Place Saint-Augustin, where she gets into another taxi. She leaves this one, still with the little boy, at the corner of the Rue Montmartre and the Grands Boulevards.

The page was ornamental, for Maigret was decorating it with drawings like a child's.

On another sheet he noted the dates on which they had lost track of the various characters:

Countess Panetti . . . *February 16*

The garage attendant at Claridge's had been the last to see her when she had stepped into her son-in-law's chocolate-colored Chrysler.

Krynker . . . ?

Maigret hesitated to write down the date Saturday, February 17, for they had no proof at all that he was the third person dropped by the taxi at the corner of the Rue de Turenne.

If that were not he, his tracks disappeared simultaneously with the old lady's.

### Alfred Moss . . . *Tuesday, March 12*

He had been the first to leave the Hôtel Beauséjour, about noon.

### Levine . . . *Tuesday, March 12*

Half an hour after the preceding character, while seeing Gloria into a taxi.

### Gloria and the child . . . *Same date*

Two hours later, in the crowd at the Carrefour Montmartre.

Today was Sunday, March 17. Since the twelfth there had been nothing new to report. Except for the investigation.

Or rather there was one date to note, which he added to the column:

*Friday, March 15*—Somebody in the métro tries (?) to pour some poison into the dinner prepared for Frans Steuvels.

But that was still in doubt. The experts had found no trace of poison. In the state of nervous exhaustion Fernande had been in recently, she might well have mistaken a passenger's clumsiness for a deliberate action.

In any case it wasn't Moss popping up again, for she would have recognized him.

Levine?

Suppose it was a message, and not poison, that some-one had tried to slip into the casserole?

Maigret, with a sunbeam catching him in the face, made a few more little drawings, screwing up his eyes, then he went to look at a string of barges going past on the Seine and at the Pont Saint-Michel, which families dressed in their Sunday clothes were crossing.

Madame Maigret had probably gone back to bed, as she sometimes did on Sundays, simply to make it seem more like Sunday, for she was incapable of going back to sleep.

"Janvier! What about ordering some beer?"

Janvier called the Brasserie Dauphine, and the pro-prietor asked as a matter of course:

"And some sandwiches?"

Through a timid telephone call Maigret discovered that Judge Dossin, punctilious, was in his office; he too, no doubt, like the chief inspector, was hoping to sort things out in peace.

"Still no news of the car?"

It was amusing to think that on this beautiful Sunday which smelled of spring, in the villages where people were coming out of Mass and out of little cafés, hard-working policemen were keeping an eye on the cars and looking for the chocolate-colored Chrysler.

"May I look, Chief?" asked Lucas, who had come to stretch his legs in Maigret's office between telephone calls.

He examined the chief inspector's work carefully, shook his head.

"Why didn't you ask me? I've drawn up the same dia-gram, in more detail."

"But without the little drawings," Maigret teased. "What's the leading item in the phone calls? Cars? Moss?"

"Cars for the moment. Lots of chocolate-colored cars. Unfortunately, when I pin them down, they're no longer exactly chocolate-colored but reddish brown or else they're

Citroëns or Peugeots. We check anyhow. The suburbs are beginning to phone in now, and the radius is expanding to about sixty miles from Paris."

In a little while, thanks to the radio, all France would be in on it. There was nothing to do but wait, and that wasn't so disagreeable. The waiter from the Brasserie brought a huge tray covered with glasses of beer and piles of sandwiches, and there was every chance that he would make more trips before the day was out.

They were in the midst of eating and drinking and they had just opened the windows, for the sun was warm, when they saw Moers come in, blinking his eyes as though he were emerging from a dark place.

They hadn't known he was in the building, where, theoretically, he had no business. And yet here he was coming from upstairs, where he must be the only person in the laboratories.

"I'm sorry to bother you."

"A glass of beer? There's one left."

"No, thanks. As I was falling asleep, an idea kept bothering me. We were so sure that the blue suit unquestionably belonged to Steuvels that we examined it only for blood-stains. As the suit's still up there, I came in this morning to do an analysis of the dust."

This was, in fact, a routine procedure which no one had thought of in the present case. Moers had sealed each piece of clothing in a strong paper bag and then he had given the bag a good beating so as to extract every trace of dust from the cloth.

"Find anything?"

"Sawdust, very fine, in remarkable quantities. It's really more like wood powder."

"The kind you might get in a sawmill?"

"No. That kind of sawdust would be less fine, less pervasive. Powder is produced by fine handwork."

"Cabinetwork, for instance?"

"Possibly. I'm not sure. It's even finer than that, in my opinion, but before I commit myself I'd like to have a word with the head lab man tomorrow."

Without waiting to hear the end, Janvier had picked up a volume of the directory and was studying all the addresses in the Rue de Turenne.

This yielded a list of various and sundry trades, some of them surprising, but by some chance nearly all connected with metals or cardboard.

"I thought I'd just mention it to you. I don't know whether it will help."

Neither did Maigret. In an investigation like this, one never knows what may help. At all events this tended to support the testimony of Frans Steuvels, who had always denied being the owner of the blue suit.

But then why did he own a blue overcoat—a poor selection to go with a brown suit?

Telephone! Sometimes six instruments would be in use at the same time, and the switchboard operator was going out of her mind, for there were not enough people to take all the calls.

"What is it?"

"Lagny."

Maigret had been there once. It is a little town on the edge of the Marne, with a lot of men fishing and shiny canoes. He couldn't remember the case he had been on, but it was in summer, and he had drunk a light white wine, the memory of which was still with him.

Lucas was taking notes, indicating to the chief inspector that this seemed serious.

"Maybe we've got hold of something," he sighed as he hung up. "That was the Lagny police. For over a month they've been quite excited down there about a car that fell in the Marne."

"It fell into the Marne a month ago?"

"As far as I could make out, yes. The sergeant I had on

the phone was so anxious to explain and go into detail that in the end I couldn't make head or tail of it any more. Besides, he kept dropping names I didn't know, as you might say Jesus Christ or Pasteur, and coming back over and over again to Old Mother Hébart or Hobart, who gets drunk every night but who is apparently incapable of making anything up.

"To cut it short, about a month ago——"

"Did he tell you the exact date?"

"February 15th."

Maigret, very proud at finding a use for it, consulted the list he had just drawn up.

*Thursday, February 15*—Countess Panetti, accompanied by her maid, Gloria Lotti, leaves Claridge's in the chocolate-colored Chrysler of her son-in-law Krynker.

"I thought of that. This looks serious, you'll see. So this old woman, who lives in an isolated house at the edge of the river and who rents canoes to fishermen in summer, went down to the tavern for a drink, as she does every evening. When she was returning home she claims that she heard a great crash in the darkness and that she's sure it was the crash of a car falling into the Marne.

"The river was in flood at the time. A minor road leading from the main highway ends at the water's edge, and the mud must have made it slippery."

"Did she report it to the police right away?"

"She talked about it in the café next day. It took some time to get around. It finally reached the ears of a policeman, who questioned her.

"The policeman went down for a look, but the banks were partly submerged, and the current was so violent that navigation had to be suspended for a couple of weeks. Apparently the level is only just now getting back to normal.

"I think the truth is that they didn't take the whole matter very seriously.

"Yesterday, after receiving our alarm on the chocolate-colored car, they had a phone call from someone who lives at the corner of the highway and the minor road in question and who claims that last month he saw, in the darkness, a car of that color turning around in front of his house.

"He's a gas station proprietor who was filling up a customer's car, which explains why he was outside at that time."

"What time?"

"Just after nine o'clock at night."

It doesn't take two hours to get from the Champs-Élysées to Lagny, but of course there was nothing to prevent Krynker from making a detour.

"And so?"

"The police applied to the Highway Department for the crane."

"Yesterday?"

"Yesterday afternoon. There was a crowd watching it work. Anyhow in the evening they caught something, but the darkness prevented them from carrying on. They even told me the name of the hole, because the river holes are well known to the fishermen and local people. There's one that's thirty feet deep."

"Did they fish the car out?"

"This morning. It really is a Chrysler, chocolate-colored, with an Alpes-Maritimes registration number. That's not all. There's a body inside."

"Male?"

"Female. It's terribly decomposed. Most of the clothing's been torn off by the current. The body is still on the bank, under a tarpaulin, and they want to know what they're to do with it. I said I'd call them back."

Moers had left a few minutes too soon, for he was the

man who would have been invaluable to the chief inspector, and there wasn't much chance of finding him at home.

"Would you call Dr. Paul?"

The latter answered in person.

"You're not busy? No plans for the day? Would it be too inconvenient if I came over and picked you up to take you to Lagny? With your bag, yes. No. It probably won't be a pretty sight. An old woman who's spent a month in the Marne."

Maigret looked around and saw Lapointe glancing away and blushing. The young man was obviously burning with the desire to accompany the chief.

"You haven't got a date for this afternoon?"

"Oh, no, Chief Inspector."

"Can you drive?"

"I've had my license for two years."

"Go and fetch the blue Peugeot and wait for me downstairs. Check the gas."

And to Janvier, disappointed:

"You take another car and drive down slowly, questioning the garagemen, wine merchants, anyone you like. It's possible that somebody else may have noticed the chocolate-colored car. I'll see you at Lagny."

He drank the extra glass of beer, and a few minutes later Dr. Paul cheerfully settled himself in the car which Lapointe was proudly driving.

"Shall I take the shortest way?"

"Preferably, young man."

It was one of the first fine days, and there were a lot of cars on the road, crammed with whole families and their picnic baskets.

Dr. Paul told stories of autopsies which, from his lips, were as funny as Jewish jokes or jokes about lunatics.

At Lagny they had to ask directions, go through the little town and make some long detours before arriving at a bend in the river where a crane was surrounded by at least a hundred people. The police were having as much trouble as if it had been fair day. An officer was on the scene and he seemed relieved to see the chief inspector.

The chocolate-colored car, covered with mud, grass and unidentifiable flotsam, was there, upside down on the bank, with water still streaming from all its cracks. Its body was all out of shape, one of the windows broken, both headlights shattered; but by an extraordinary chance one door was still working, and through this they had extricated the body.

It formed a little heap under the tarpaulin which no sight-seer could approach without his stomach turning.

"I'll leave you to it, Doctor."

"Here?"

Dr. Paul would have been willing to do it. With his eternal cigarette in his mouth, he had been known to carry out autopsies in the most unlikely places, even to stop and take off his rubber gloves in order to eat a snack.

"Can you take the body to the police station, Lieutenant?"

"My men will see to it. Stand back, everybody. And the children! Who's letting children come so close?"

Maigret was examining the car when an old woman plucked him by the sleeve and said proudly:

"It was me who found it."

"Are you Widow Hébart?"

"Hubart, sir. That's my house that you can see behind the ash trees."

"Tell me what you saw."

"I didn't see anything actually, but I heard. I was coming back along the towing path. That's the path we're on."

"Had you had a lot to drink?"

"Only two or three."

"Where were you?"

"Fifteen feet from here, farther on, nearer my house. I heard a car coming in from the highway and I said to myself it must be poachers again. Because it was too cold for lovers, and it was raining into the bargain. All I saw, when I turned around, was the beam from the headlights.

"I didn't know that this was going to be important someday, did I? I kept on walking and I had the impression that the car had stopped."

"Because you couldn't hear the motor any more?"

"Yes."

"You had your back to the road?"

"Yes. Then I heard the motor again and I thought the car was turning around. Not a bit of it! Immediately afterward there was a big 'plouf' and when I looked around the car was gone."

"You didn't hear any shouting?"

"No."

"You didn't turn back?"

"Should I have? What could I have done all by myself? It had upset me. I thought the poor people had been drowned and I hurried home to get a drink to revive me."

"You didn't stay by the water's edge?"

"No, sir."

"You didn't hear anything after the 'plouf'?"

"I thought I heard something, footsteps maybe, but I decided it must be a rabbit frightened by the noise."

"Is that all?"

"Don't you think it's enough? If they'd listened to me instead of treating me like a crazy old fool, the lady would have been out of the water long ago. Have you seen her?"

Not without a grimace of disgust, Maigret imagined this old woman contemplating the other decomposed old woman.

Did the Widow Hubart realize that it was a miracle she was still alive and that if her curiosity had impelled her to turn back on that notable evening she would probably have followed the other woman into the Marne?

"Won't the reporters be coming?"

That's what she was waiting for—to have her picture in the papers.

Lapointe, covered with mud, was climbing out of the Chrysler, which he had examined.

"I didn't find a thing," he said. "The tools are in their place in the trunk, with the spare tire. There's no luggage; no handbag. There was only a woman's shoe caught in the back of the seat, and in the glove compartment this pair of gloves and this electric flashlight."

The pigskin gloves were men's, so far as one could tell.

"Go over to the railway station. Someone must have taken the train that night. Unless there are any taxis in town. Meet me at the police station."

He preferred to wait in the courtyard, smoking his pipe, until Dr. Paul, installed in the garage, had finished his task.

# 8

## THE TOY FAMILY

"ARE YOU DISAPPOINTED, Monsieur Maigret?"

Young Lapointe was longing to say "Chief," like Lucas, Torrence and most of the rest of the team, but he felt too much of a newcomer for that. It seemed to him that this was a privilege he would have to earn, like winning one's spurs.

They had just driven Dr. Paul home and were on their way back to the Quai des Orfèvres, in a Paris which seemed to them more luminous after the hours spent floundering in the darkness of Lagny. From the Pont Saint-Michel Maigret could see the light in his own office.

"I'm not disappointed. I wasn't expecting the railway employees to remember passengers whose tickets they punched a month ago."

"I was wondering what you had in mind."

He replied quite naturally:

"The suitcase."

"I swear it was in the studio the first time I went to the bookbinder's."

"I don't doubt it."

"I'm positive it wasn't the same suitcase that Sergeant Lucas found that afternoon in the basement."

"I don't doubt that either. Leave the car in the yard and come up."

From the animation of the few men on duty it was clear that something had happened, and Lucas, hearing Maigret come back, hastily opened his office door.

"Some information on Moss, Chief. A young lady and her father came in earlier. They wanted to speak to you personally, but after waiting almost two hours they decided to give me the message. The young lady's a pretty girl of sixteen or seventeen, plump and rosy, who looks you frankly in the eye. The father's a sculptor who, if I got it straight, once won the Prix de Rome. There's another girl a bit older and a mother. They live on the Boulevard Pasteur, where they manufacture toys. If I'm not mistaken, the young lady came along with her father to prevent him from stopping for a drink, which seems to be his besetting sin. He wears a big black hat and a flowing cravat. Moss, going by the name of Peeters, has been living in their house for the last few months."

"Is he still there?"

"If he were I'd already have sent some detectives over to arrest him, or rather I'd have gone myself. He left them on March 12."

In other words, the day Levine, Gloria and the child disappeared from circulation after the scene in the Place d'Anvers park.

"He didn't tell them he was leaving. He went out in the morning as usual and hasn't set foot in the apartment since. I thought you'd prefer to interrogate them yourself. Oh, and something else. Philippe Liotard has telephoned twice already."

"What does he want?"

"To speak to you. He asked if you'd call him at the Chope du Nègre if you came in before eleven."

Maigret knew the tavern on the Boulevard Bonne-Nouvelle.

"Get me the Chope."

It was the cashier who answered. She had the lawyer paged.

"Is that you, Chief Inspector? I expect you must be swamped with work. Have you found him?"

"Who?"

"Moss. I went to the movies this afternoon and I caught on. Don't you think a personal, off-the-record conversation might be useful to us both?"

It happened quite by chance. A little earlier, in the car, Maigret had been thinking about the suitcase. And then, while Liotard was talking to him, little Lapointe entered the office.

"Are you with friends?" the chief inspector asked Liotard.

"It doesn't matter. When you get here I'll leave them."

"Your lady friend?"

"Yes."

"No one else?"

"Somebody you're not very fond of—why, I don't know —and who's very distressed about it."

It was Alfonsi. They must have made up a foursome again, the two men and their girls.

"Would you have the patience to wait for me if I'm a bit late?"

"I'll wait as long as you like. It's Sunday."

"Tell Alfonsi I'd like to see him too."

"He'll be charmed."

"See you soon."

He went and closed the two doors to his office, telling Lapointe, who out of tact was about to leave, to stay.

"Come here. Sit down. You want to get ahead in the police, don't you?"

"More than anything else."

"You made the stupid mistake of talking too much the

first day, and this has had consequences which you don't even suspect yet."

"I'm sorry. I had complete confidence in my sister."

"Do you want to try something difficult? Just a moment. Don't be in too much of a hurry to answer. It's not a matter of a glorious stunt that will get you your name in the papers. Quite the contrary. If you succeed, nobody but us two will ever know about it. If you mess it up, I shall be obliged to disclaim all responsibility and maintain that you were acting on your own hook outside my orders."

"I understand."

"You don't understand at all, but that doesn't matter. If I were to take the job on myself and fail, the whole of the police force would be involved. You're new enough here to get away with it."

Lapointe could not contain his impatience.

"Maître Liotard and Alfonsi are at the Chope du Nègre at the moment, where they're waiting for me."

"Are you going to join them?"

"Not right away. First I want to make a call in the Boulevard Pasteur, and I'm sure they won't budge from the tavern before I get there. Suppose I go and join them in an hour at the earliest. It's nine o'clock. You know where the lawyer lives, on the Rue Bergère? It's the fourth floor left. As a number of young ladies live in the house, the concierge probably doesn't pay too much attention to who comes and goes."

"You want me to . . ."

"Yes. You've been taught how to open a door. It won't matter if you leave marks. Quite the contrary. No sense in going through drawers and papers. You're to make sure of just one thing; that the suitcase isn't there."

"I never thought of that."

"All right. It's possible and even probable that it isn't there, because Liotard is a cautious chap. That's why you mustn't waste any time. From the Rue Bergère you're to go straight over to the Rue de Douai, where Alfonsi has Room 33 in the Hôtel du Massif Central."

"I know."

"Do the same thing there. The suitcase. Nothing else. Call me as soon as you're through."

"Can I leave now?"

"Go out into the corridor first. I'm going to lock my door and you try to open it. Ask Lucas for the tools."

Lapointe didn't do too badly and a few minutes later he was hurrying out, utterly overjoyed.

Maigret went in to the inspectors.

"Are you free, Janvier?"

The telephones were still going but, because of the time of night, with less virulence.

"I was giving Lucas a hand, but . . ."

They went downstairs together, and it was Janvier who took the wheel of the little police car. A quarter of an hour later they reached the quietest, least brightly lighted stretch of the Boulevard Pasteur, which, in the peace of a beautiful Sunday evening, looked like the main avenue of some small town.

"Come up with me."

They asked for the sculptor, whose name was Grossot, and were directed to the seventh floor. The building was old but very well kept, probably inhabited by minor government employees. When they knocked at the door of the seventh-floor apartment the sound of an argument suddenly ceased and a young girl with full cheeks opened the door and stepped back.

"Was it you who came to my office earlier?"

"That was my sister. Chief Inspector Maigret? Come in. Pay no attention to the mess. We're only just finishing dinner."

She led them into a huge studio, with a sloping ceiling, partly glass, beyond which the stars could be seen. There were the remains of some cold cuts on a long pine table, an open liter of wine. Another girl, who looked like the twin of the one who had opened the door, was tidying her hair with a furtive movement, while a man in a velvet jacket approached the visitors with exaggerated solemnity.

"Welcome to my modest abode, Monsieur Maigret. I hope you will do me the honor of taking a drink with me."

Since leaving Police Headquarters the old sculptor must have managed to get something to drink besides table wine, because his speech was impaired, his gait unsteady.

"Don't pay any attention," interposed one of the girls. "He's got himself in that state again."

She said this without rancor, and the look she gave her father was affectionate, almost maternal.

In the darkest corners of the great room pieces of sculpture could be vaguely sensed, and it was clear that they had been there for a long time.

More recent, part of their present life, were the carved wooden toys lying around on the furniture and filling the room with a good smell of fresh wood.

"When art no longer offers a living to a man and his family," Grossot was declaiming, "there's nothing to be ashamed of—is there?—in looking to commerce for one's daily bread."

Madame Grossot appeared; she must have gone to tidy up when she heard the bell. She was a thin woman, sad, with constantly watchful eyes, who must always be foreseeing misfortunes.

"Won't you give the chief inspector and this gentleman a chair, Hélène?"

"The chief inspector knows perfectly well that he can make himself at home here, Mother. Don't you, Monsieur Maigret?"

"Didn't you offer him anything?"

"Would you like a glass of wine? There's nothing else in the house on account of Papa."

She seemed to be the one who controlled the family; at

all events the one who was taking control of the conversation.

"We went to the movies yesterday, in this neighborhood, and we recognized the man you're looking for. He was using the name Peeters, not Moss. The reason we didn't come to see you earlier was that Papa hesitated to turn him in and protested that he had been our guest and eaten at our table several times."

"Had he been living here long?"

"About a year. The apartment takes up the whole floor. My parents have lived here more than thirty years, and I was born here and so was my sister. There are three rooms besides the studio and the kitchen. Last year the toys didn't bring in much, and we decided to take a boarder. We put an advertisement in the paper.

"That's how we got to know Monsieur Peeters."

"What did he say his profession was?"

"He told us that he represented a big English mill and that he had his own customers so there was no need for him to go out much. Sometimes he'd spend the whole day at home and come and give us a hand, in his shirt sleeves. Because we all work on the toys, for which my father makes the models. Last Christmas we got an order from the Printemps and we worked night and day."

Grossot was eying the half-empty wine bottle so pathetically that Maigret said to him:

"Oh, well, pour me half a glass, just for the sake of having a drink with you."

He received in return a look of gratitude, while the girl continued, without taking her eye off her father to be sure he didn't help himself too freely:

"He usually went out toward the end of the afternoon and he would sometimes come home quite late. Occasionally he would take his sample case with him."

"Did he leave his luggage here?"

"He left his big trunk."

"Not his suitcase?"

"No. By the way, Olga, did he have his suitcase when he left?"

"No. He didn't bring it back last time he took it out with him."

"What kind of man was he?"

"He was quiet, very gentle, perhaps rather sad. Sometimes he would stay shut up in his room for hours at a time, and in the end we'd go and ask if he was ill. Other times he'd have breakfast with us and help us all day.

"Occasionally he would disappear for several days and he would tell us beforehand not to worry about him."

"What did you call him?"

"Monsieur Jean. He called us by our first names, except my mother, of course. He would sometimes bring us candy, little presents."

"Never expensive presents?"

"We wouldn't have accepted them."

"He never had visitors?"

"Nobody ever came. He never got any mail either. I was surprised that a businessman shouldn't receive any letters, and he explained to me that he had a partner downtown, with an office, and his correspondence was addressed there."

"Did he ever seem odd to you?"

At this she glanced around and murmured, though without emphasis:

"Well, here, you know!"

"Your health, Monsieur Maigret. To your investigation! As you can see, I no longer count for anything, not only in the domain of art but even in my own house. I don't protest. I say nothing. They're very nice, but for a man who——"

"Let the chief inspector talk, Papa."

"You see?"

"You don't know when your boarder went out with his suitcase for the last time?"

It was Olga, the older girl, who answered:

"The last Saturday before . . ."

She debated whether she ought to continue.

"Before what?"

The younger child reassumed control of the interview.

"Don't blush, Olga. We're always teasing my sister because she had a crush on Monsieur Jean. He wasn't the right age for her and he wasn't handsome, but . . ."

"What about yourself?"

"Never mind that, Olga. One Saturday, about six o'clock, he went out with his suitcase, which was surprising in itself because it was usually on Mondays that he took it with him."

"Monday afternoons?"

"Yes. We weren't expecting him back, thinking he was going away for the weekend somewhere, and we were making fun of Olga, who was moping."

"That's not true."

"We haven't the slightest idea what time he came home. Usually we'd hear him open the door. On the Sunday morning we thought his room was empty and we were just talking about him when he came out, looking ill, and asked my father if he would mind getting him a bottle of brandy. He said he'd caught cold. He stayed in bed part of the day. Olga, who takes care of his room, noticed that the suitcase wasn't there. She noticed something else—at least she claims she did."

"I'm sure of it."

"You may be right. You looked at him more closely than we did."

"I'm sure his suit wasn't the same one. It was a blue suit too, but not his, and when he had it on I noticed that it was a bit too big on the shoulders."

"He didn't say anything about it?"

"No. We didn't mention it either. After that he complained that he was coming down with the flu and stayed at home for a whole week without going out."

"Did he read the papers?"

"The morning and evening paper, just as we do."

"You didn't notice anything out of the ordinary?"

"No. Except that he'd go and shut himself up in his room the minute anybody knocked at the door."

"When did he start going out again?"

"About a week later. The last time he slept here was the night of March 11. That's easy to be sure of because on the calendar in his room the leaves haven't been torn off since then."

"What ought we to do, Chief Inspector?" asked the mother anxiously.

"I don't know, madame."

"If the police are looking for him . . ."

"May we have a look at his room?"

It was at the end of a passage. Spacious, not luxurious but clean, with old waxed furniture and reproductions of Michelangelo on the walls. An enormous black trunk of the most common kind was in the right-hand corner, tied up with cord.

"Open it, please, Janvier."

"Shall I go out?" asked the girl.

He didn't see any necessity. Janvier had more trouble with the cord than with the lock, which was commonplace. A strong smell of mothballs pervaded the room, and suits, shoes, underwear began to pile up on the bed.

It might have been an actor's wardrobe, judging by the range of quality and origin in the clothing. A set of tails and a dinner jacket bore the label of a big London tailor, and another dress suit had been made in Milan.

There were also some white linen suits of the kind worn mainly in hot countries; some pretty loud outfits; others which, on the contrary, might have belonged to a bank teller; and for all of them there were matching shoes, bought in Paris, Nice, Brussels, Rotterdam or Berlin.

Finally, at the very bottom, separated from the rest by a sheet of brown paper, they unearthed a clown's costume, which the girl stared at in more bewilderment than the rest of them.

"Was he an actor?"

"In his own way."

There was nothing else revealing in the room. The blue suit they had just been talking about wasn't there, for Peeters-Moss was wearing it when he left; perhaps he was still wearing it.

In the drawers, small objects: cigarette cases, wallets, cuff links and studs, keys, a broken pipe, but not one document, no address book.

"Thank you, mademoiselle. It was very sensible of you to inform us and I'm sure you won't regret it. I suppose you haven't a telephone?"

"We used to have one a few years ago, but . . ."

And in a low voice:

"Papa hasn't always been like this. That's why we can't hold it against him. He used not to drink at all. Then he met some old friends from the Beaux Arts who are just about in the same boat, and he got into the habit of going out with them to a little café in the Saint-Germain section. It didn't do them any good."

A bench in the studio held several precision tools for sawing, gluing and planing the tiny pieces of wood from which they made miniature toys.

"Take along a bit of sawdust in a paper, Janvier."

This would please Moers. It was amusing to think that through his analysis alone they would inevitably have made their way in the end to this apartment perched high in a building on the Boulevard Pasteur. It would have taken weeks, possibly months, but they would have got there just the same.

It was ten o'clock. The wine bottle was empty, and Grossot proposed to accompany "these gentlemen" down to the street, which he was not permitted to do.

"I'll probably be back."

"And the other one?"

"I don't expect so. In any case I don't think you have anything at all to fear from him."

"Where shall I drop you, Chief?" asked Janvier, taking the wheel of the car.

"Boulevard Bonne-Nouvelle. Not too near the Chope du Nègre. Wait for me."

It was one of those big taverns that serve sauerkraut and frankfurters, where on Saturday and Sunday evenings four half-starved musicians play on a dais. Maigret immediately spied the two couples not far from the front window; noted that the two ladies had ordered green crème de menthe.

Alfonsi was the first to stand up, not completely sure of himself, like a man who expects a kick in the pants, while the lawyer, smiling and self-possessed, held out his well-kept hand.

"May I introduce our girl friends?"

He did so condescendingly.

"Would you like to sit down for a minute at this table or do you want to move over to a separate one right away?"

"On condition that Alfonsi keeps the ladies company and waits for me, I'd rather hear what you have to say now."

A table was vacant near the cash desk. The clientele was mainly made up of local shopkeepers treating their families to dinner in a restaurant, just as Maigret had done the night before. There were also some regular customers: bachelors or unhappily married men, playing cards or checkers.

"What will you have? A beer? One beer and one brandy and water, waiter."

It would probably not be long before Liotard was frequenting bars near the Opéra and the Champs-Élysées, but for the present he still felt more at home in this neighborhood, where he could stare at people with an air of great superiority.

"Has your alarm brought any results?"

"Was it to question me, Maître Liotard, that you invited me to come and see you?"

"Maybe it was to make peace. What would you say to that? Perhaps I was a bit short with you. Don't forget that we're on opposite sides of the fence. Your job is to bear down on my client; mine is to save him."

"Even by becoming his accomplice?"

The shot went home. The young lawyer with the long, pinched nostrils blinked two or three times.

"I don't know what you mean. But if that's the way you want it, I'll come straight to the point. As luck has it, Chief Inspector, you're in a position to do me a lot of harm, even to delay, if not interrupt, a career which everyone agrees will be brilliant."

"I don't doubt it."

"Thank you. The Bar Association is pretty strict about certain rules, and I admit that in my hurry to get ahead I haven't always stuck to them."

Maigret was drinking his beer with the most innocent air in the world, watching the cashier, and she might have mistaken him for the hatmaker from the shop around the corner.

"I'm waiting, Maître Liotard."

"I hoped you might help me, because you know very well what I'm referring to."

He still did not react.

"You know, Chief Inspector, I come from a poor family, very poor——"

"The Counts Liotard?"

"I said very poor, not commoners. I had a hard time paying my way through law school and when I was a student I had to take all kinds of jobs. I even wore a uniform in a big movie theater downtown."

"Congratulations."

"Even a month ago I wasn't eating every day. I was waiting, like all my colleagues of my own age and some older ones too, for a case that would give me a chance to distinguish myself."

"You found it."

"I found it. That's what I'm getting at. On Friday, in Monsieur Dossin's office, you uttered certain words which made me think that you knew a great deal about this business and that you wouldn't hesitate to use it against me."

"Against you?"

"Against my client, if you prefer."

"I don't understand."

Of his own accord Maigret ordered another beer, for he had rarely drunk any as good, especially in contrast to the sculptor's lukewarm wine. He was still watching the cashier, as if he was glad she looked so much like old-fashioned café cashiers, with her big bust pushed up by her corset, her black silk blouse ornamented with a cameo, her hair like a set piece in a hairdresser's window.

"You were saying?"

"All right, if that's the way you want it. You're determined to make me come clean and you've got the whip hand. I made a professional error in soliciting Steuvels to become my client."

"Only one?"

"I happened to hear about the whole thing in a perfectly routine way and I hope no one is going to have any trouble on my account. I'm quite friendly with a certain Antoine Bizard; we live in the same building. We've been through the mill together. We've been reduced to sharing a can of sardines or a camembert. Recently Bizard got a steady job on a paper. He has a girl friend."

"The sister of one of my detectives."

"So you do know."

"I like hearing you tell it."

"Through his job on the paper—he's a leg man—Bizard is in a position to hear about certain matters before they become public."

"Crimes, for instance."

"If you like. He's gotten into the habit of calling me."

"So that you can go over and offer your services?"

"You're a cruel winner, Monsieur Maigret."

"Go on."

He was still looking at the cashier and at the same time making sure that Alfonsi was keeping the two women company.

"I was informed that the police were interested in a bookbinder in the Rue de Turenne."

"On February 21, early in the afternoon."

"That's right. I went over there and I really did talk about a bookplate before bringing up a hotter matter."

"The furnace."

"That's all. I told Steuvels that if he was in any trouble I'd be glad to defend him. You know all that. And it was not so much for my own sake that I instigated the conversation we've had tonight, which I hope will remain strictly between the two of us, as for my client's. Anything that would harm me at the moment would harm him by repercussion. There it is, Monsieur Maigret. It's for you to decide. I may be suspended from the Bar tomorrow morning. All you have to do is go and see the President and tell him what you know."

"Did you stay at the bookbinder's long?"

"Fifteen minutes at the most."

"Did you see his wife?"

"I think at one point she stuck her head out of the stair well."

"Did Steuvels take you into his confidence?"

"No. I'll give you my word of honor on that."

"One more question, Maître. How long has Alfonsi been working for you?"

"He's not working for me. He's running a private detective agency."

"Of which he's the only employee!"

"That's none of my business. To defend my client with any chance of success I need certain information which it would be unbecoming for me to dig up for myself."

"Primarily you needed to be kept up to date on what I know."

"That's fair enough, isn't it?"

The cashier picked up the telephone, which had just rung, and answered:

"Just a minute. I don't know. I'll find out."

And as she opened her mouth to give a name to the waiter the chief inspector stood up.

"Is it for me?"

"What's your name?"

"Maigret."

"Do you want to take it in the booth?"

"Never mind. I'll only be a second."

It was the call he was expecting from young Lapointe. The latter's voice was tense with excitement.

"Is that you, Chief Inspector? *I've got it!*"

"Where?"

"I didn't find anything at the lawyer's, where I nearly got caught by the concierge. I went over to the Rue de Douai as you had told me. There were crowds of people going in and out there. It was easy. I had no trouble opening the door. The suitcase was under the bed. What shall I do with it?"

"Where are you?"

"At the cigar store on the corner of the Rue de Douai."

"Take a taxi to the Quai. I'll meet you there."

"Yes, *Chief*. Are you pleased?"

Carried away by his enthusiasm and pride, he was venturing the expression for the first time—though not with complete confidence.

"You've done a good job."

The lawyer was watching Maigret uneasily. The chief inspector sat down again at his place on the banquette with a sigh of satisfaction and signaled to the waiter.

"Another beer. It might be a good idea to bring this gentleman a brandy."

"But . . ."

"Pipe down, boy."

This made the lawyer gasp with indignation.

"Look, it's not the Bar Association I'm going to report you to. It's the Public Prosecutor. Tomorrow morning I'll probably ask him for two warrants for arrest, one in your name, one in that of your crony Alfonsi."

"Are you kidding?"

"What's that likely to get you—suppression of evidence in a murder case? I'll have to look up the statute book. I'll think it over. May I leave the check to you?"

Already on his feet, he added softly, confidentially, leaning over Philippe Liotard's shoulder:

"I've got the suitcase!"

# 9

## THE DIEPPE SNAPSHOT

MAIGRET HAD CALLED the judge's office the first time at about half past nine and spoken to the clerk.

"Would you ask Monsieur Dossin if he can see me?"

"Here he is now."

"Something new?" the judge had asked. "I mean besides what's in the morning press?"

He was very excited. The papers reported the discovery of the chocolate-colored car and the body of the old woman at Lagny.

"I think so. I'll come and tell you about it."

And since then, every time the chief inspector made for the door of his office something had delayed him—a telephone call or the arrival of a detective who had a report to make. The judge had called back discreetly and asked Lucas:

"Is the chief inspector still there?"

"Yes. Shall I put him on?"

"No. I suppose he's busy. I'm sure he'll be up in a minute."

At a quarter past ten he had finally made up his mind to get Maigret on the line.

"Sorry to bother you. I imagine you're swamped. But

143

I'm having Frans Steuvels brought in at eleven o'clock and I wouldn't want to begin the interrogation before seeing you."

"Would you mind if your interrogation turned into a confrontation?"

"Who with?"

"With his wife, probably. If I may, I'll get a detective to bring her in just on the chance."

"Do you want a regular confrontation?"

"That won't be necessary."

Monsieur Dossin waited a good ten minutes more, pretending to study the dossier. At last there was a knock at the door. He almost made a rush for it and saw Maigret silhouetted, a suitcase in his hand.

"Are you going away?"

The chief inspector's smile enlightened him, and he murmured, not able to believe his eyes:

"The suitcase?"

"It's heavy, I can tell you."

"So we were right?"

He was relieved of a great weight. The systematic campaign of Philippe Liotard had finally shaken him, and it was he, after all, who had taken the responsibility of keeping Steuvels in prison.

"Is he guilty?"

"Guilty enough to be put inside for several years."

Maigret had known the contents of the suitcase since the previous evening, but he made the inventory again, with all the pleasure of a child setting out his Christmas presents.

What made the brown suitcase with the handle mended with string so heavy were some pieces of metal which looked a bit like bookbinder's stamps but were actually the seals of various sovereign states.

Conspicuous among them were those of the United States and of all the South American republics.

There were also some rubber stamps like those used in

city halls and government offices, all arranged as carefully as a traveling salesman's samples.

"Steuvels' work," explained Maigret. "His brother Alfred provided him with the models and the blank passports. As far as I can tell from these specimens, the passports weren't counterfeit but were obtained by theft from the consulates."

"Had he been in this business long?"

"I don't think so. Two years roughly, judging by the bank accounts. In fact this morning I telephoned most of the banks in Paris, and that's partly what kept me from coming up to see you earlier."

"Steuvels has an account at the Société Générale in the Rue Saint-Antoine, hasn't he?"

"He has another in an American bank in the Place Vendôme, and another in an English bank on the boulevard. So far we've found five different accounts. It began two years ago, which corresponds with the date when his brother came back to Paris to live."

It was raining. The weather was gray and mild. Maigret sat by the window, smoking his pipe.

"You see, Monsieur le Juge, Alfred Moss doesn't fall into the category of professional criminals. Those men have one specialty, and most of the time they stick to it. I've never known a pickpocket to turn burglar or a burglar to kite checks or try the confidence game.

"Alfred Moss is a clown, first and foremost, an acrobat.

"It was as a result of a fall that he got into this business. If I'm not greatly mistaken he brought off his first job by chance when, cashing in on his knowledge of languages, he was hired by a big London hotel as an interpreter. An opportunity arose to steal some jewelry, and he seized it.

"This was enough for him to live on for a time. Not for long, because he has one vice—I found this out this morning too, from his local bookie—he plays the horses.

"Like any amateur, he didn't stick to one type of theft; he wanted to try everything.

"He did it with unusual skill and luck, since it's never been possible to prove anything against him.

"He had his ups and downs. The confidence game would follow check kiting.

"He wasn't as young as he used to be; he was known to the police in most capitals, blacklisted in the big hotels where he regularly operated."

"That's when he remembered his brother?"

"Yes. Two years ago the gold traffic, which had been his previous activity, wasn't paying off any more. On the other hand, faked passports, especially for America, were beginning to bring astronomical prices. He figured that a bookbinder, accustomed to reproducing coats of arms by means of stamps and blocks, would be able to do just as good a job with official seals."

"What amazes me is that Steuvels, who doesn't lack for anything, should have accepted. Unless he leads a double life which we haven't discovered."

"He doesn't lead any double life. Poverty—real poverty of the kind he knew in his childhood and adolescence— produces two kinds of people: free spenders and misers. It more often produces misers, and they're so afraid of seeing the bad days return that they're capable of anything at all to provide against them.

"If I'm not greatly mistaken, that's the case with Steuvels. The list of banks where he's made deposits offers additional proof. I'm convinced this wasn't just a way of hiding his nest egg, because it never occurred to him that he might be found out. But he was suspicious of banks and of nationalization and devaluation and he would put by a bit here and a bit there, in different banking houses."

"I thought he practically never went out without his wife."

"That's right. It was she who went out without him, and

it took me some time to discover that. On Monday afternoons she went to the Vert-Galant laundry barge to do her washing. Almost every Monday Moss would come over with his suitcase and when he was early he'd wait at the Tabac des Vosges until his sister-in-law had left.

"The two brothers had the afternoon before them for their work. The tools and the compromising documents never remained at the Rue de Turenne. Moss took them away with him.

"On some Mondays Steuvels would even have time to hurry over to one of his banks and make a deposit."

"I don't see what part was played by the young woman with the child or by Countess Panetti or——"

"I'm coming to that, Monsieur le Juge. I told you about the suitcase first because that's what bothered me more than anything else right from the start. Ever since I knew of the existence of Moss and suspected what he was up to, I've had another question on my mind.

"Why, on Tuesday, March 12, all of a sudden, when the gang seemed quiet, was there an unusual flare-up which ended in its dispersing?

"I mean the incident in the Place d'Anvers park which my wife happened to witness.

"Only the night before, Moss was living peacefully in his furnished room on the Boulevard Pasteur.

"Levine and the child were staying at the Hôtel Beauséjour, where Gloria would come and pick up the child every morning to take him for a walk.

"Now, on that Tuesday, about ten in the morning, Moss enters the Hôtel Beauséjour, where, probably as a precaution, he has never set foot.

"Immediately Levine packs, dashes over to the Place d'Anvers, calls Gloria, who deserts the child in order to follow him.

"By the afternoon they've all disappeared, leaving no trace.

"What happened on the morning of March 12?

"Moss couldn't have received a telephone call because the house he lives in has no telephone.

"Neither I nor my detectives made any move at that moment that might have alarmed the gang, the existence of which we didn't even suspect.

"As for Frans Steuvels, he was in the Santé.

"All the same, something did happen.

"And it was only last night, when I went home, that through the wildest chance I found the answer to this question."

Monsieur Dossin was so relieved to know that the man he had put in prison was not innocent that he was listening with a sort of fascinated smile, as he might have listened to a joke.

"My wife had been waiting for me all evening and had spent the time catching up on a little job she takes care of now and again. This consists of keeping scrapbooks of all newspaper clippings that mention me, and she does it more devotedly than ever since a former commissioner of police published his memoirs.

" 'You might possibly write yours someday, after you've retired and when we live in the country,' she'll reply when I make fun of her hobby.

"In any case, when I got home last night, the scissors and paste were on the table. While I was making myself comfortable I happened to glance over my wife's shoulder and in one of the clippings she was just pasting in I saw a photo which I had completely forgotten.

"It had been taken three years ago by a little journalist in Normandy. We were spending a few days at Dieppe, and he'd caught us—my wife and myself—on the steps of our *pension*.

"What amazed me was to see this photo on a page from an illustrated magazine.

" 'Didn't you read it? It came out recently—a four-page

article on the early days of your career and your methods.'

"There were some other photographs, one of me when I was a precinct secretary and had a drooping mustache.

" 'What's the date of it?' I asked her.

" 'Of the article? Last week. I haven't had time to show it to you. You've hardly been home lately.'

"In short, Monsieur Dossin, the article had appeared in a Paris weekly which went on sale on the morning of Tuesday, March 12.

"I immediately sent someone over to see the people Moss was still living with on that date, and they confirmed that the younger of the girls had taken the magazine in to him, with the milk, at about half past eight, and that Moss had glanced at it while he was having breakfast.

"From then on everything's straightforward. This even explains Gloria's long sessions on the park bench in the Place d'Anvers.

"After their two murders and the arrest of Steuvels, the gang, now broken up, was lying low. Levine probably changed hotels several times before moving into the Rue Lepic. For safety he never appeared with Gloria outside, and they even went so far as to avoid spending the night in the same place.

"Moss must have come to the Place d'Anvers every morning to keep in touch, and all he had to do was take a seat at the end of the bench.

"Now, as you know, my wife sat down three or four times on that same bench before her dentist's appointment. The two women had gotten acquainted and would chat. Moss had probably seen Madame Maigret, to whom he hadn't paid any attention.

"Imagine his reaction when he found out from the magazine that the good lady on the bench was none other than the wife of the chief inspector in charge of the investigation!

"He couldn't believe it was accidental, could he? He

quite naturally thought that we were on his track and that I had turned over this delicate bit of sleuthing to my wife.

"He rushed over to the Rue Lepic and alerted Levine, who dashed over to warn Gloria."

"What was the argument about?"

"Perhaps about the child. Perhaps Levine didn't want Gloria to go back for him, thus running the risk of being arrested. She insisted on going, but with maximum precautions.

"This also makes me inclined to think that when we find them again they won't be together. They'll figure that we know Gloria and the boy, while we know nothing about Levine. He must have gone off in one direction and Moss in another."

"Do you expect to catch them?"

"Maybe tomorrow, maybe a year from now. You know how things go."

"You still haven't told me where you found the suitcase."

"Perhaps you would prefer not to know *how* we got possession of it! I was, in fact, forced to use slightly illegal methods, for which I take sole responsibility, but you couldn't possibly approve them.

"All you need to know is that it was Liotard who relieved Steuvels of the compromising suitcase.

"For one reason or another, on the Saturday night Moss had taken the suitcase to the Rue de Turenne and left it there.

"Frans Steuvels had simply shoved it under a table in his workshop, thinking no one would bother about it.

"On February 21 Lapointe invented a pretext to be admitted and searched the place.

"Remember that Steuvels couldn't get in touch with his brother or any other member of the gang, probably, to let them know what was going on. I have a theory about that.

"He must have wondered how to get rid of the suitcase and was doubtless waiting until after dark to see about it, when Liotard, whom he'd never heard of, turned up."

"How did Liotard get to know?"

"Through an indiscretion in my department."

"One of your detectives?"

"I don't blame him for it, and there's not much chance that it will ever happen again. In any case Liotard offered his services, even going a bit beyond what one is entitled to expect from a member of the Bar, since he disposed of the suitcase."

"Did you find it at his place?"

"At Alfonsi's. He'd passed it on to him."

"Where do we stand now?"

"Nowhere. I mean, we know nothing about the essential thing—the two murders. A man was killed in the Rue de Turenne, and previously Countess Panetti was killed in her car—where, we don't know. You must have received a report from Dr. Paul, who found a bullet in the old lady's cranium.

"However, a small item of information has reached me from Italy. More than a year ago the Krynkers were divorced in Switzerland, since divorce is impossible in Italy. Countess Panetti's daughter regained her liberty to marry an American, with whom she is now living in Texas."

"There was never a reconciliation with her mother?"

"On the contrary. Her mother was more furious with her than ever. Krynker is a Hungarian of good family but poor. He spent part of the winter at Monte Carlo, trying to make his fortune at gambling—without succeeding.

"He arrived in Paris three weeks before the death of his ex-mother-in-law and lived at the Commodore, then in a small hotel on the Rue Caumartin."

"How long had Gloria Lotti been in the old lady's service?"

"Four or five months. That hasn't been determined exactly."

A sound was heard in the corridor, and the usher came to announce that the prisoner had arrived.

"Am I to tell him all this?" asked Monsieur Dossin, whose responsibilities were weighing on him again.

"There are two possibilities: either he'll talk or he'll keep on refusing to. I've had dealings with several men from Flanders in my time and I've learned that they're hard to soften up. If he won't talk it will take weeks— possibly longer. We'll have to wait, in fact, until we rout out one of the four characters holed up Lord knows where."

"Four?"

"Moss, Levine, the woman and the child, and our best bet may be the child."

"Unless they've got rid of him."

"If Gloria went back for him when he was in my wife's charge, she must be attached to him."

"Do you think it's her son?"

"I'm sure of it. It's a mistake to think criminals aren't like other people, that they can't have children and love them."

"Her son by Levine?"

"Probably."

Rising to his feet, Dossin smiled a faint smile with a trace of mischief and of humility too.

"This would be the time for a 'grilling,' wouldn't it? Unfortunately that's not my strong point."

"If you'd allow me, perhaps I might talk to Liotard."

"To get him to advise his client to talk?"

"As matters stand now, it's in their interest—both of them."

"Shall I have them brought in right away?"

"In a moment."

Maigret went out and said cordially to the man sitting to the right of the door, on the bench worn smooth by constant use:

"Good morning, Steuvels."

Just at that moment Janvier was coming out into the corridor, together with a very distressed Fernande. The inspector was doubtful about letting the woman join her husband.

"You have time for a chat together," Maigret said to them. "The judge isn't quite ready."

He made Liotard a sign to follow him, and they talked in undertones, pacing up and down the murky corridor, where there were policemen outside most of the doors. It took barely five minutes.

"When you're ready, just knock."

Maigret went into Monsieur Dossin's office alone, leaving Liotard, Steuvels and Fernande in conversation.

"Result?"

"We'll see. Liotard's going along, obviously. I'll cook you up a nice little report in which I'll mention the suitcase without emphasizing it."

"Isn't that a bit irregular?"

"Do you want to catch the murderers?"

"I understand you, Maigret. But my father and my grandfather were on the Bench, and I think I'll end my days there too."

He was blushing, waiting for a knock on the door with a mixture of impatience and misgiving.

At last it opened.

"Shall I bring Madame Steuvels in too?" asked the lawyer.

Fernande had been crying and had her handkerchief in her hand. She immediately tried to catch Maigret's eye to give him a look of distress, as though she felt confident that he could still put everything right.

Steuvels for his part hadn't changed. He was still wearing the expression that was both gentle and stubborn at the same time, and he went and sat down obediently on the chair he was motioned to.

As the clerk was about to take his place Monsieur Dossin said to him:

"Wait. I'll call you when the interrogation becomes official. Are you agreeable, Maître Liotard?"

"Quite, thank you."

Maigret was the only one standing up now, facing the window, down which little raindrops were rolling. The Seine was gray like the sky; the barges, the roofs, the sidewalks reflected the wetness.

Then, after two or three little coughs, Judge Dossin's voice was heard, saying diffidently:

"I believe the chief inspector would like to put a few questions to you, Steuvels."

Maigret, who had just lighted his pipe, had no alternative but to turn around, trying to suppress a smile of amusement.

"I suppose," he began, still standing up, as if he were addressing a class, "your counsel has briefly given you the picture. We know what you and your brother have been up to. Possibly, so far as you personally are concerned, we may have nothing else to charge you with.

"It was not, in fact, your suit which showed traces of blood, but that of your brother, who left his suit with you and took yours away with him."

"My brother didn't commit murder either."

"Probably not. Do you want me to interrogate you, or would you rather tell us what you know?"

Not only was Maître Liotard on his side now, but Fernande, by the look in her eyes, was urging Frans to talk.

"Question me. I'll see if I can answer."

He wiped the thick lenses of his glasses while he waited, round-shouldered, head slightly bent forward as if it were too heavy.

"When did you learn that Countess Panetti had been killed?"

"In the course of Saturday night."

"You mean the night when Moss, Levine and a third person, who is probably Krynker, came to your house?"

"Yes."

"Was it your idea to send a telegram to get your wife out of the way?"

"I wasn't even told about it."

This was plausible. Alfred Moss was sufficiently familiar with the couple's domestic habits and way of life.

"So when someone knocked at your door about nine o'clock that evening you didn't know what it was about?"

"Yes. Anyhow I didn't want to let them in. I was reading peacefully in the basement."

"What did your brother tell you?"

"That one of his companions needed a passport that same evening and he'd brought everything along and I'd better get to work."

"Was that the first time he'd brought strangers to your house?"

"He knew I didn't want to see anyone."

"But you knew he had accomplices?"

"He'd told me he was working with a man named Schwartz."

"The man who called himself Levine at the Rue Lepic? A rather fat man, very dark?"

"Yes."

"You all went down to the basement together?"

"Yes. I couldn't work in the workshop at that time of night or the neighbors would have wondered what was up."

"Tell me about the third man."

"I don't know him."

"Did he have a foreign accent?"

"Yes. He was a Hungarian. He seemed anxious to get away and he kept on asking if he wouldn't run into trouble with a false passport."

"For what country?"

"The United States. They're the hardest to fake because of certain special marks known only to the consuls and the Immigration Service."

"So you started work?"

"I didn't have time."

"What happened?"

"Schwartz was inspecting the apartment, as if he was making sure no one could take us by surprise. Suddenly, while I had my back turned—I was bending over the suitcase, which was standing on a chair—I heard a shot and saw the Hungarian slumping to the floor."

"Was it Schwartz who had fired?"

"Yes."

"Did your brother seem surprised?"

A moment's hesitation.

"Yes."

"What happened next?"

"Schwartz maintained that this was the only possible way out and that it wasn't his fault. According to him, Krynker had lost his nerve and would inevitably have been caught. If he'd been caught, he would have talked.

" 'I was wrong to treat him like a man,' he added.

"Then he asked me where the furnace was."

"He knew there was one?"

"I think so."

Through Moss, obviously; as it was obvious also that Frans did not want to inculpate his brother.

"He ordered Alfred to start a fire and asked me to bring some very sharp tools.

" 'We're all in the same boat, boys. If I hadn't shot down this idiot we'd have been arrested within a week. Nobody saw him with us. Nobody knows he's here. He has no family to start making inquiries. Let's get him out of the way and we'll be all right.' "

This wasn't the moment to ask the bookbinder if they had all helped with the dismemberment.

"Did he tell you about the old lady's death?"

"Yes."

"Was this the first you'd heard of it?"

"I hadn't seen anybody since the point where they left in the car."

He was becoming more reticent, while Fernande's glance was traveling from her husband's face to Maigret's.

"Speak out, Frans. They got you into it and then left you holding the bag. What good is it going to do you to keep quiet?"

Maître Liotard was adding:

"In my capacity as your counsel, I can tell you that it's not only your duty to speak out but in your own interest too. I think the court will take your frankness into consideration."

Frans looked at him with big worried eyes and shrugged his shoulders slightly.

"They spent part of the night at my place," he finally brought out. "It took a very long time."

A sudden heave of her stomach made Fernande put her handkerchief to her mouth.

"Schwartz—or Levine, never mind his name—had a bottle of brandy in his overcoat pocket, and my brother drank a lot.

"At one point Schwartz said to him, looking furious:

" 'That's the second time you've pulled this one on me.'

"And that was when Alfred told me the story of the old lady."

"Just a minute," interrupted Maigret. "What exactly do you know about Schwartz?"

"He was the man my brother was working for. He had talked to me about him several times. He thought he was pretty tough, but dangerous. He has a child from a pretty girl, an Italian, whom he lives with most of the time."

"Gloria?"

"Yes. Schwartz worked mainly in the big hotels. He'd

got on to a very rich, eccentric woman and he expected to get a lot out of her, and he'd made Gloria take a job as her maid."

"And Krynker?"

"I really only saw him dead, because the shot was fired when he'd only been in my house a few moments. There are some things I didn't understand until later, when I thought about it."

"For instance?"

"That Schwartz had prepared the whole thing in minute detail. He wanted to get Krynker out of the way and he'd hit upon this method of getting rid of him without running any risk. When he came to my house he knew what was going to happen. He'd sent Gloria to Concarneau to send off the telegram to Fernande."

"And the old lady?"

"I wasn't mixed up in that episode. I only know that since his divorce Krynker, who was on the coast, had tried to get in touch with her. Recently he succeeded, and she would sometimes give him small amounts of money. This would immediately melt away, because he liked to live high. What he wanted was enough money to get to the United States."

"Was he still in love with his wife?"

"I don't know. He met Schwartz, or rather Schwartz, tipped off by Gloria, managed to meet him in a bar, and they became more or less friendly."

"Was it on the night of Krynker's death and the furnace that they told you all this?"

"We had to wait hours while——"

"Yes, yes."

"I wasn't told whether it was Krynker's idea or whether Schwartz suggested it to him. Apparently the old lady was in the habit of traveling with a case containing jewelry worth a fortune.

"It was about the time of year when she regularly went

to the Riviera. It was just a matter of inducing her to go in Krynker's car.

"On the way, at a prearranged point, the car would be attacked and the jewel case stolen.

"In Krynker's mind this was to be managed without bloodshed. He was convinced that he wasn't running any risk since he would be in the car with his ex-mother-in-law.

"For some reason or other Schwartz fired, and I think he did it on purpose because this put the other two at his mercy."

"Your brother too?"

"Yes. The attack took place on the Fontainebleau road, and afterward they drove as far as Lagny to get rid of the car. Schwartz lived in a cottage somewhere near there at one time and was familiar with the district. What else do you want to know?"

"Where are the jewels?"

"They found the case all right, but the jewelry wasn't in it. Probably the countess had her suspicions after all. Gloria, who was with her, knew nothing about it either. Maybe she left them in a bank."

"That's when Krynker lost his head?"

"He wanted to try to get across the frontier right away, on his own papers, but Schwartz insisted he'd be caught. He wasn't sleeping at all and drinking a lot. He was bordering on panic, and Schwartz decided that the only way to get any peace at all was to get rid of him. He brought him to my house on the pretext of obtaining a false passport for him."

"Why was your brother's suit——"

"At one point Alfred stumbled, exactly where——"

"So you gave him your blue suit and kept his and cleaned it the next day?"

Fernande's head must have been full of bloody pictures. She was looking at her husband as though seeing him for the first time, no doubt trying to imagine him during the days and nights he had subsequently lived through alone in the basement and in the workshop.

Maigret saw her shudder, but the next moment she held out a hesitant hand, which finally came to rest on the bookbinder's big paw.

"Perhaps they have a bindery in prison," she said, making an effort to smile.

\*\*\*

Levine, whose name was not Schwartz or Levine but Sarkistian and who was wanted by the authorities of three countries, was arrested a month later in a little village near Orléans, where he was spending his time fishing.

Two days later Gloria Lotti was found in a brothel at Orléans and she steadfastly refused to reveal the name of the peasants to whom she had entrusted her son.

As for Alfred Moss, his description remained on the police wanted list for four years.

One night, in a little circus which was traveling from village to village along the roads of the *département* of Nord, a down-at-heel clown hanged himself, and from an examination of the papers found in his suitcase the police discovered his identity.

Countess Panetti's jewels had not left Claridge's, having been locked up in one of the trunks left in the baggage room; and the shoemaker in the Rue de Turenne never admitted, not even when he was dead drunk, that it was he who had written the anonymous letter.